BORN AMONG THE DOLPHINS

PATRICK

Lagrou

BORN AMONG THE DOLPHINS
WITHDRAWN

Clavis

First published in Belgium and Holland by Clavis Uitgeverij, Hasselt – Amsterdam, 2002
Copyright © 2002, Clavis Uitgeverij

English translation from the Dutch by Clavis Publishing Inc. New York
Copyright © 2008 for the English language edition: Clavis Publishing Inc. New York

Visit us on the web at www.clavisbooks.com

Born Among the Dolphins written by Patrick Lagrou
Original title: *Het dolfijnenkind*
Translated from the Dutch by Hanny Veenendal
Edited by Erin Harte

ISBN: 978 1 60537 022 4

Manufactured in the USA
First Edition
10 9 8 7 6 5 4 3 2 1

PROLOGUE

Thursday evening, June 25

Under a tropical starry sky, a luxurious sailing yacht cut its engine and slowly came to a stop preparing to moor. The yacht belonged to Harold Thompson, a fabulously wealthy banker from New York. It arrived in Key Largo, the first in a string of islands south of Florida. Less than a hundred yards away, the streetlights reflected beautifully in the calm waters.

The ship drifted quietly to the middle of the bay. A young man stood at the bow waiting to drop the anchor in the water at the signal. It was his first visit to this tropical part of the United States.

His eyes scanned the dark water. Then, suddenly, he saw a triangular fin cutting through the reflection of the street lamps dancing on the surface of the water.

"Shark!" he yelled. "There's a big shark swimming around the ship!" His cries did not go unnoticed. One of the deckhands burst outside and immediately spotted the infamous triangle.

"I'll take care of that right away!" he said.

The man stormed back into the pilothouse and grabbed the rifle they kept on board for emergencies. With Harold Thompson, himself, aboard, the crew couldn't take any chances. You never knew what could happen on a ship. Last winter, modern day pirates raided several yachts sailing in the Caribbean.

Three shots rang out into the quiet evening air. A dozen pelicans flew up, startled. The water briefly splashed, and red slowly stained the surface of the ocean.

At the exact moment the shots were fired, across the country in Madison, Wisconsin, a twelve-year-old boy awoke screaming.

"Mou-Mou! No! No! Don't! Don't go away! Mou-Mou! Mou-Mouuuuu!"

Michael O'Neil shivered after his dream. Something really terrible had happened. But whoever this 'Mou-Mou' was, he could only guess.

Within thirty seconds, Michael's mother rushed into his small bedroom. From her own room, Patricia O'Neil had heard Michael's shouts loud and clear. Immediately, she understood that her son's cries had a profound meaning: the past was coming back to life.

ONE

"Now this is very important," Mr. Powell said, leaning on his desk for emphasis.

The whole class listened intently.

"Christopher Columbus caught sight of the first island of the New World on Friday, October 12th, 1492," said Mr. Powell. "And he landed that same day on the island of San Salvador. Unfortunately, we have no way of knowing precisely where this happened, not by miles and miles. Fifty years ago, they put up a big stone cross on a beach there, but there's no guarantee that it's the exact spot where Columbus actually landed."

A few students looked at the picture of the cross on the screen behind Mr. Powell and seemed disappointed.

"However," their history teacher exclaimed enthusiastically, "the situation is completely different with the third island Columbus landed on five days later. Because he described the whole area in his log, down to the smallest details. That's why we could easily locate this spot. See, look!"

On the screen in front of the class, an enormous satellite photo appeared. Mr. Powell pointed to a deep bay, at the entrance of which was a tiny island

"Well," said the teacher, "on Wednesday, October 17th, Columbus anchored his three ships close by. He sailed into the bay with a small boat, and a little while later, he set foot ashore. And there, from the beach, he saw a river emptying into the ocean …"

The teacher turned around, and pointed out the location of the river on the fuzzy satellite photograph.

"But there isn't a river there!" a voice said from the front of the classroom. "Columbus must have made a mistake!"

All eyes were on a single boy in one of the front row seats. They all knew him, because for the umpteenth time this year, Michael O'Neil just had to make a comment. He had a habit of paying very close attention to the lessons. But as soon as Michael heard a detail that was at odds with something his teacher had said earlier, or with a fact he'd read in a book, he pointed it out for the class. Michael O'Neil had an amazing memory. Many of his teachers were weary of his comments because most of the time, he was actually right. It was a good thing that Michael was also in the habit of speaking in a very friendly manner. Although this time he had sounded quite rude.

Mr. Powell restrained himself. He tried to approach the boy as diplomatically as he could.

"Now why do you think that, Michael?" he asked in a friendly tone. "Are you suggesting that not only am I wrong, but that Christopher Columbus, of all people, is wrong as well? You must feel extremely confident." While uttering this last sentence, the teacher had not been able to prevent a note of mockery in his voice. Immediately, he regretted it because some of the students started snickering. He fervently hoped Michael would come up with a rock solid answer, or this time he would make himself the laughingstock of the class.

"Well," Michael said, after some hesitation, "I really don't know why, but that whole area seems very familiar." Never before had Michael O'Neil come up with such a lame answer. Everybody in the classroom was aware of it. Today, it looked as if he had gone too far. This time, they had him!

"Maybe you've been there?" Mr. Powell offered, trying to help. When he saw the whole class was beginning to really enjoy this spectacle, the Mr. Powell started to feel sorry for Michael.

"I don't think so," Michael answered, "but I'm sure it's not a river."

"What else have you been dreaming up?" one of the kids in the row behind Michael asked, making fun of him.

Everybody started laughing.

8

"I'm not dreaming ..." Michael cried out, furiously. "It's true! Because instead of a river, there's a swamp with a little bridge across ..."

"And Columbus built the bridge, too?" another student yelled.

The whole class was roaring with laughter. Michael crouched down and didn't say a word.

All Mr. Powell could do, was shake his head sympathetically. He had never seen Michael O'Neil like this before. What could have gotten into that boy?

The front door slammed shut. Patricia O'Neil knew right away that something was wrong with her son. Usually, Michael came home in a good mood. His voice would sound full of enthusiasm: he'd had such an interesting day at school; he'd learned so much fun stuff. Her son's cheerful attitude had always been such a relief to Patricia. These past years, hadn't been easy for her.

For more than ten years, Patricia had practically been on her own. Her family had never forgiven her for the "mistake" she had made when she was younger. It was especially hard during that first year in Boston when Patricia had very little money. Even though she graduated from a good school, no employer would hire her; her powerful relatives made sure of that. Patricia had had to bury her grand ideas for the future because in the end, her dreams had given her nothing but problems and misery.

Patricia then realized that she would only find peace and prosperity if she broke radically with her past. She was quick in making a big decision: she packed-up and moved to Madison, Wisconsin. Here was a town that accepted her for who she was. She quickly found an interesting job as a teacher. From then on, her future looked decidedly rosy.

At the same time, Patricia made another decision: she would never, under any circumstances, allow her past to influence her life, or her son's life, again, in any possible way. She would devote herself completely to Michael. She didn't need a new partner; Michael would get all her attention; she would raise him to be the man of her dreams, so that later on in life, she would be able to look up to him.

In the following years, Michael certainly did not disappoint her. In fact, it was quite the opposite. Michael was a model student from day one. He was somewhat withdrawn, but that could be blamed on the fact that he didn't have a father. And maybe that was why he took such an interest in the world of the grown-ups. He couldn't wait to be a part of their world. And he was making good progress – except when his over eagerness put him on the opposite side of the rest of his class, which had obviously happened again today.

Patricia O'Neil quickly sensed that something had gone wrong in school. She could see from the look on Michael's face that the kids had made fun of him today. But she knew how to help him to get over it quickly. Her son was usually right. Her job was to show him that being right wasn't the same as being convincing. And, to explain to him that being right wasn't even that important. Usually, his anger faded when she talked to him this way. But she didn't realize that this time it was a very different situation.

"And when I told them it was a swamp with a little bridge, the whole class was laughing at me," Michael exploded. "But Mom, I'm sure that that's how it is. I couldn't have dreamed it, could I have? Do you think I did?"

With mounting horror, Patricia listened to her son's story. Now that he asked her opinion, she didn't know how to answer him. Especially after what had happened last night.

"Darling," she said, "this time, I can't tell you you're right. You must have been dreaming. That's all I can say." To prevent Michael from questioning her further, she got up and left the room. Patricia O'Neil had never been this abrupt with her son, but after all, she didn't have a choice.

Across town, Mr. Powell entered his study. The history teacher grabbed a tube standing in the corner next to his monumental bookcase that contained a military survey map of the northern part of Long Island in the Bahamas. He had debated between using this map or the satellite photo for today's class. In the end, he'd picked the photo. It may not have been a close view, but it was real. But now he could certainly use the survey map. Especially after his exchange with Michael today. If Mr. Powell was lucky, he would soon know for sure whether or not Michael had been right. The teacher was curious what the boy had been thinking.

Very carefully, Mr. Powell pulled the rolled-up map from the tube and unfolded it. Along the top, he looked for the site where Columbus had landed all these years ago. He quickly found the bay in question. From there, his gaze wandered to the supposed location of the river. But what had looked like a river on the blurry satellite photo turned out to be nothing but a mangrove marsh on the map. And across its narrowest part, there was a little bridge.

"My goodness," Mr. Powell exclaimed, "Michael was right after all. But how on earth could he have known?"

TWO

It was almost ten o'clock when Patricia turned off the light on her night-stand; her room was suddenly pitch black. She couldn't sleep if the light from the street lamps shined through the windows into her room, which was why Patricia hung dark curtains on her bedroom windows the first day they moved into their new home. The only other thing that could keep her from falling asleep was the ticking of the alarm clock. But usually, she was so tired that it didn't really disturb her.

But now sleep wouldn't come. The ticking was getting on her nerves. In the past twenty-four hours, two things had happened with Michael that she hadn't expected. After all these years, she'd thought the past was finally dead and buried. And now, all of a sudden, it had reared its head, and more fiercely than ever. Naturally, Patricia felt badly about leaving Michael in the dark. But, in spite of everything, she didn't want to undo her decision to never look back.

For now, peace and quiet seemed to have been restored. But how long would that last? Michael had often shown that he had a phenomenal memory. And even though his deepest memories were hidden beneath a thick layer of dust, it obviously didn't take much for them to resurface. Especially after what had happened last night. After all, it had been more than ten years since Michael had used the word: 'Mou-Mou'. It brought Patricia right back to those days in the hospital. There she had gone through something similar, more than once. She was so afraid to lose him. Was it starting all over again?

That same day, the Miami Herald ran the following story:

Gipsy Killed by Accident

Key Largo has lost its mascot. Gipsy, a tamed dolphin who had been living in the area for years, was shot last night around 10:00 PM by a passenger on a yacht. The shooter, an artist from New York, thought he had seen a shark. With a rifle, he fired three shots at the animal. One of the shots hit Gipsy in the chest and proved fatal.

Gipsy was a 20-year-old female dolphin. She had been living in the Key Largo area for more than six years. She had a scar below her right eye, which made it easy to recognize her. Gipsy was a welcome guest up and down the beaches. She often swam into shallow waters to play with the children. Toddlers and kindergartners were especially fond of her. In her death, Key Largo has lost a great playmate for its kids.

For more information on this special dolphin and for testimonies and reactions, please see our weekend edition.

THREE

Monday, June 29th

The shouts and cries of the students were deafening in the aquarium auditorium. One group after another poured into the cavernous space. The kids ran up the bleachers as fast they could. Everyone wanted the best seat in the house.

Michael sat by the stairs at the end of one of the rows, hunched over and quiet. He was one of the first ones there. He couldn't wait for the show to begin; he'd been looking forward to this day for such a long time.

The field trip had started very early that morning. The boy was relieved when the bus was finally able to leave. Now he was out of his mother's reach. Since Michael found out about the trip, he hadn't mentioned it at home. He hid all the information about it. Under no circumstances did he want his mother to know that he would be seeing dolphins today. She wouldn't have let him go. Michael didn't know why, but he knew his mother had something against these animals. Every time he started talking about them, she would change the subject as if she were afraid of it. Michael, on the other hand, thought dolphins were the coolest animals he could imagine. Very often, he dreamed he was swimming with them under water. And those dreams seemed so real. And so incredibly beautiful. Except, of course, that nightmare last week …

Last weekend, Michael had gone to the library again. There he secretly read books on dolphins. He wondered why his mother was so opposed to dolphins. She was scared of everything that concerned water. For instance, he was the only one of his classmates who wasn't allowed to take swimming classes. He couldn't even go to the swimming pool with the others. When he was younger, the doctors had said Michael wasn't allowed to swim. That was all his mother had told him. And yet, as soon as Michael saw a swimming pool, he felt the urge to dive right in. He didn't feel the least bit scared.

And now, directly in front of him was this giant water basin. Through the glass walls he could see all the way down to the bottom. He was excited by this humongous blue tank. Even more so as the time passed because he knew that in just a few minutes real dolphins would be swimming around in there. Michael could hardly believe it was going to happen.

Suddenly, there was music and all the kids started clapping. The host of the program walked into the big space. In one hand he held a wireless microphone, with the other he waved.

"A good afternoon, boys and girls," he called. "Welcome to our dolphin show."

The host sat down on a small platform and introduced himself and the trainers. Then he said a few things about the aquarium and its inhabitants.

Michael started to get impatient. He hoped it wouldn't be long before the dolphins made an appearance. Finally, it looked as if they were coming. But he was mistaken. From a water basin in the back, a large seal swam forward. The animal did a few tricks that Michael thought were okay. But after a while, he was bored. The performance was basically just a string of silly jokes. The trainer played a dumb clown while the seal constantly outwitted her. That was all right for little kids, Michael thought, but not for him. The dolphin show better be a whole lot more interesting. Finally, applause filled the auditorium and the seal slid back into his familiar basin. Michael stared intently at the little passageway on the right side. He was certain the first dolphins would come out from that side, he could feel it.

However, the host just droned on and on. He talked for so long that minutes seemed like hours. Finally, the show began. An assistant pulled up a trapdoor and the dolphins came swimming in. Everybody cheered, except Michael. He looked at the animals with wide eyes. Suddenly, he started shivering all over his body as if he was in the middle of an ice-cold storm. His shivering became more severe as the animals slid back and forth behind the glass wall. When the dolphins jumped up high in the air for the first time and dove back deep into the water, Michael's whole body was shaking. The boy did not know what was happening to him. Strange forces had been unleashed in him and were slowly taking possession of his body. And his mind, too. Michael was losing track of where he was. His eyes latched onto the dolphins as they swam back and forth, back and forth.

At one point, one of the dolphins hesitated as if it had caught on to something. It was no longer swimming in synch with the others, but bobbing at the surface. Its snout kept changing direction. It was like a sniffing dog that caught a scent, but couldn't make out which direction it was coming from. Then the dolphin started moving. The animal swam to the edge of the basin and, through the glass wall, looked straight at Michael. As if it saw someone he knew, the dolphin began squealing non-stop. At that same moment, the other dolphins also stopped performing their tricks. They followed the example of the first dolphin.

The two trainers blew their whistles and tried to get the attention of the animals with a couple of fish. It didn't work. Even the host, who had been narrating the events the whole time, was at a loss for words. Only the piped-in music kept playing. The audience, who had not caught on yet, thought it was just a joke and was laughing.

Michael stood up. The boy had no idea what was going on, but he felt as though the dolphins were calling him. All he could do was to listen to them.

Step by step, he walked down the stairs, stiff and straight with his eyes focused on the dolphins that were looking at him. Immediately, Michael became the center of attention. Through the microphone, the host asked the boy to return to his seat. But Michael did not respond and slowly continued descending the stairs.

Almost all the kids in the bleachers thought it was a joke and started laughing even harder. Only Michael's classmates were no longer laughing. They did not understand at all what was happening. Puzzled, they looked at Mr. Powell, who by now had gotten up from his seat. Stepping over all the children's legs, he tried to get to the other side of the row.

Michael reached the tank. The dolphins saw him standing on the other side of the glass. They became very spirited. Then the boy jumped up. Like a monkey, Michael climbed up the transparent wall to the upper rim of the tank. Mr. Powell ran after Michael, but couldn't catch him in time.

The children howled with laughter. The host kept repeating that Michael should stop climbing and come down. But it was as if the boy could not hear anything or anyone. It seemed that Michael was totally unaware that he was messing everything up.

And then it happened. With a big splash, Michael jumped in the water, smack into the middle of the group of dolphins. Most of his classmates' hearts skipped a beat, and they were scared to see what would happen next. Michael, who, as far as they knew, had never learned how to swim, was now in the deep water. But their fear quickly gave way to surprise. Michael was patting one dolphin after another as if they were old friends. And after that, none of the students could believe their eyes. Even Mr. Powel thought he was dreaming.

Michael held onto the back fin of one of the dolphins, and then disappeared under water, accompanied by the other animals. The kids could watch him through the glass wall. They saw how Michael and the dolphins reached the bottom at a depth of fifteen feet and swam through the blue water for more than a minute. When he finally resurfaced, the audience applauded like crazy. Then the trainers and the host stared as Michael went under again. They had lost all control over their animals. They just stood by, bewildered. They wanted to do something, but didn't know what, or how.

Again the crowd burst into applause; Michael was sitting on the back of a dolphin. They had lost count of how many times he'd gone under water. This was a show none of the kids could have ever imagined. And if the water in the tank had been warmer, the show would have lasted even longer.

But Michael started to get cold. Surrounded by the animals, he moved to the edge of the basin. There he was roughly caught by the scruff and hauled up from the water. And right away, the spell was broken. And at the same time, Michael started to realize what he had done …

"I'll pick him up right away and bring a set of dry clothes."

Patricia put down the telephone. This was it. The inevitable had happened. For ten years, she'd hoped that the past would remain buried, but today it had risen with all its might. There was no use denying it. Hundreds of people had seen it happen. Tonight the whole school would know, and it might even be in the papers tomorrow. She knew there would be a barrage of questions. Michael would certainly demand an explanation. The forces that she hoped had vanished were apparently still with him. For years they'd waited to break out. Today, however, was the first time it had happened again.

And maybe this was only the beginning. Lots of other things could happen. And she had to prevent that one way or the other. She would have to tell Michael everything. And the best place to do that was the place where he came from.

Patricia was aware that she was facing a very difficult task, but there was no escaping it. Now she was relieved that it was almost vacation time and that Michael would be away from school for a long time.

FOUR

Sunday, August 2, a little after 9:00 in the morning

The Greyhound bus slowed down and entered Chicago's bus terminal. Michael got ready to get off. Just thirty more minutes on another bus and they would finally be at the airport.

He had gotten up at four when it was still dark. His mom had never hauled him out of bed so early. But unlike other mornings, it didn't take much talking to get him up. Michael had been looking forward to this day for weeks. After the adventure in the aquarium, Michael initially feared he would be severely punished. But things turned out very differently. His mom hadn't even been mad. In fact, it was just the opposite – she took responsibility for everything. And just a few days later, she had made the travel plans.

"Michael, you'll be thirteen this summer," she said. "I would rather have waited a few more years, but the past has apparently caught up with you. There are a number of things you need to know. You used to ask me why we were different than most other people. You also wanted to know why you didn't have a father anymore. Each time I told you that strange things had happened in the past, and that your father had suddenly disappeared. I promised I would tell you more when you were older when you could understand these things better. I'm afraid that time has come, much sooner than I had hoped. From now on, you'll learn everything, bit by bit, because if you hear the whole story at once, it may be too much for you to handle. And to help you understand even better, we're going on a trip. We'll go down to the place where it all started. It will be a kind of pilgrimage for both of us. I'll show you everything, so you will experience it all first hand."

After these last words, Patricia let out a great big sigh. She felt a heavy burden lifted off her shoulders. From now on, she could share her big secret with someone else. But that didn't stop Patricia from being afraid of what might still be in store for them. She hoped it wouldn't be an avalanche.

Ever since the first week of July, she had gone from one travel agency to the next. She knew it would be difficult to get inexpensive tickets on such short notice. In the end, she managed to find a good deal. Since she couldn't find a direct flight, they would have to make a stopover in Atlanta. From there, it was a two-hour flight south. Once they arrived in the capital Nassau, Patricia wanted to make the rest of her trip on her own. The travel agency said it would be better to book a flight, but Patricia thought it was way too expensive; she wanted to take a boat to the island. A customer traveling to the Bahamas and continuing the trip by boat? Now there was something the travel agents didn't come across every day.

Patricia was tremendously relieved when they handed her the tickets. It was too bad it would be another three weeks before they could leave. Michael jumped for joy when he heard he was going to the Caribbean in August. Except for a couple of weeks at the beach or in the woods, he hadn't been anywhere exciting in the last few years and he'd never been on a plane before. He'd listened to his classmates' stories with envy at the beginning of the school year. They had all traveled with their parents to Canada, to the East Coast, or even to Florida. And now, all of a sudden, he was going to the Bahamas, just like Christopher Columbus had at one time. It was almost too much of a good thing. But Michael also understood that this trip would be so much more than just some kind of educational school trip. He was going to a place where a piece of him had been left behind. And even though he could hardly wait to go, he did feel a tiny bit anxious because this awesome trip might turn out to have some difficulties of its own.

Those difficulties started at the beginning of the trip. His mom told him the trip would start with a lot of standing in line and waiting, but Michael hadn't imagined it would be this bad.

The main terminal of Chicago's airport was completely full of travelers. Everybody lugged huge suitcases and bags.

"Are all those people traveling with us?" Michael asked.

"Not all of them," his mom said. "People have all kinds of different destinations. Look at that big announcement board up there. That tells you all the flights. You can see the flight number, destination, time of departure and whether or not the flight is delayed."

"Oh yeah, I get it," Michael said. "It says Atlanta, but look …"

"Our plane has a two hour delay," Patricia said.

"What? We're gonna have to wait two more hours before we can go?"

"Maybe even longer. With these cheap flights, you never know."

"We could have slept a couple more hours this morning."

"Yes, Michael, that would have been great, but that's not how it works. Let's go and see if we can get something to drink. I'm thirsty."

Patricia looked around to find the cafeteria. Everything reminded her of her first trip to the Bahamas. That was fourteen years ago. She had had a lot more luggage at that time. Then, her plan had been to stay away for at least three months. But it turned out to be almost four years …

"There are no seats here either," Michael called. When they came to the cafeteria, the boy knew they wouldn't be staying long. The place was packed. There wasn't an empty table or seat in sight.

Then they heard an announcement.

"Passengers to Atlanta, please proceed to the check in counter. Passengers to Atlanta …"

"Come on Michael, this way. Things are speeding up. As soon as we check in those suitcases, it'll be easier to move around. Maybe we can go back and get something to drink then."

FIVE

With engines roaring, the plane prepared for take off. Through the small window Michael saw the grass along the runway passing faster and faster. Then the machine lifted its nose and suddenly, Michael was flying. His big trip finally had begun.

After half an hour they heard a sound, and the lights that told people to keep their seatbelts fastened, were turned off.

"We've reached a high enough altitude now," Patricia said to Michael. "We're almost eight miles up in the sky."

"And how long are we going to fly like this?" Michael asked.

"It'll be at least another hour before the pilot will start to descend. We have plenty of time for a very long story. I have an awful lot to tell you."

Patricia pushed a button on the right side of her seat. The back reclined somewhat, so she was a bit more comfortable. Michael followed her example, but with him it did not go as smoothly. When he was settled, Patricia began.

"It all started about a year before you were born. At that time I met the man who would later become your father. I had graduated about a month before."

"How old were you?"

"Twenty two and I wanted to travel and see the world. For four years I'd been studying literature. I dreamed about becoming a journalist. I wanted to work for a magazine that would send me all over to cover all kinds of interesting issues. For me, that could've been here in our own country, or at the other end of the world."

"Wow, that's so exciting!" Michael exclaimed.

"Yes, I thought so too, but that's not how it turned out. In those first weeks, I couldn't get a job anywhere. My parents wanted me to start teaching, which I could do with my degree, but that didn't appeal to me," Patricia said.

"Is that why they never wanted to see us?"

"Not right away. That was mainly because of what happened later. Just when my father, who had a lot of influence, found me a great teaching job, I met your father."

"How did that happen?"

"Well, I saw a very interesting ad in a magazine. A biologist who studied sea animals was looking for a reporter to go with him on his next big trip. He was especially interested in dolphins."

Michael felt a jolt going through his body. He perked up his ears even more.

"A British friend of his told him there was a group of dolphins living close to one of the Caribbean islands. It would be easy for him to study them out there. He'd been waiting for an opportunity like that for years. He wanted to get there as soon as possible, but he couldn't do it on his own. That's why he had placed the ad in a scientific journal."

"And you wrote to him."

"Exactly. He invited me for an interview at New York University."

"How did that go?"

"Very well. From the very first moment, we felt we were on the same wave length. It wasn't long before he hired me. I would go with him on his trip and would be working for him the whole time. I was expected to assist with his dolphin studies, and most importantly, to keep a log of the scientific data. I also had to write a report of the journey, which I could publish later on. It sounded wonderful."

"So what was my dad's name and what was he doing at this university?"

"His name was Ben Jansen. He was doing research up until I met him. He taught a few classes sometimes when he had to substitute for one of the professors, but he thought teaching was boring. For years, he'd wanted to study dolphins out at sea. When he finally got the chance, he didn't waste any time. In late August of that same year, we flew out to the Bahamas together. The dolphins he had his eye on, were living in a bay by Long Island, one of the islands in the Bahamas."

Upon hearing the name, Michael again felt himself shiver all over. It was as if a new piece of the puzzle was put into place. But his mom kept on talking.

"I still remember the moment we arrived in Nassau, the capital. It was the height of the rainy season. When I got out of the plane, the water was coming down in buckets. I tried to run into the airport as fast as I could, but I got soaked anyway. Your father, on the other hand, cheerfully stepped down the stairs and danced in the rain. He was so happy to be away from the chilly north. He was the last passenger to walk into the building, and he looked like a drowned cat, but he couldn't have cared less." Patricia smiled.

"Tell me Mom, what did he look like?"

"When I first met him, he looked very neat. He was a tidy athletic guy who always wore a white lab coat. But the moment we arrived in the tropics, he started to loosen up, both in his manners and in the way he looked. Wait a minute, let me get some pictures. I dug them up especially for you."

Patricia freed her wallet from her purse and took out two wrinkled photographs.

Michael felt his heart beating much faster. The first photo was a portrait, an enlarged passport picture really. For the first time in his life, he saw his father's face. He immediately recognized certain features. He noticed his own wide cheekbones in his father's face. The second picture made him laugh.

"Your hair looked really funny then!" he exclaimed.

In the second picture, there were two people next to a palm tree, both wearing t-shirts and shorts. In spite of her unusual hairdo, Michael recognized his mother right away. The man standing beside her with his arm around her shoulder was not very tall, but power-fully built. He looked at least ten year older than his mom.

"When was the second picture taken? Were you engaged by then?"

"Well, Michael" Patricia laughed. "As you can see, by that time, we were more than just friends. But, where were we?"

"You'd just gotten off the plane and you were both soaking wet."

"Yes, right. Well, as soon as we could leave the airport, we drove down to Nassau's harbor in an open truck where we got drenched for the second time. Your dad had sent the stuff for the expedition a week before by air freight. Then we took a mail boat where we sailed into a big storm. During the crossing, I noticed for the first time that your dad was someone you could count on."

Michael beamed. So far, his Mom had said only nice things about his father. He secretly hoped it would stay that way. Yet, deep inside, he was full of doubts. Maybe later he would learn some things about his father that might be less pleasant.

Patricia continued her story.

"The *Day Queen*, the little mail boat we were riding, had just set sail when a tropical storm hit. The tiny, wooden ship bobbed up and down on the waves. In no time, almost everyone was sick. Only the crew and your father felt fine and kept up their spirits. I was in my bunk, sick as a dog and really embarrassed. But your father never left my side. He was constantly trying to help me: wiping my face, giving me water to drink, and telling me how brave I was. The storm lasted more than half the day. We'd left at midnight on the *Day Queen*, and it wasn't until the next afternoon that the storm stopped and the water was finally calm again. By the time we finally got to Long Island, there wasn't even a breeze. But not long after that, I desperately wished for the wind to return."

"Why was that?" Michael asked, surprised.

"Because of the sand fleas."

"The sand fleas?"

"Yes, you'll get to know them too. Wait until we arrive. Before you even see them, you'll feel them. They are tiny little bugs that bite viciously, and then you'll itch like crazy. As long as there's wind, they leave you alone, but when the wind completely dies down, they attack by the dozens."

"Can we do something about them?"

"You can wear long sleeves and long pants, but it's hot and humid like a sauna. That was the first thing I did when we arrived at Long Island. And I had just finished putting on all these clothes when there was another downpour."

"Is the weather always that bad, Mom?"

"No, fortunately it isn't, but the rainy season lasts from mid-August until around mid-November. During that time, there's at least one or more heavy shower a day. The rest of the year is dry; there's hardly a drop of rain."

"Can plants grow there?"

"Of course! All of the Bahamas is covered with thick brush and shrubs that you can hardly walk through. They call it 'the bush.' The plants that grow there absorb enormous quantities of water during the rainy season. They store it to get through the dry season. Hold on a minute – I'll show you a brochure with some photos of the Bahamas."

Patricia rummaged through her purse and took out a colorful leaflet. She opened it, so Michael could see a map with beautiful pictures.

"Mom, are those islands very large?"

"Mostly they aren't," Patricia answered. "The largest ones are only about eighty miles long and maybe a few miles wide. In fact, they're a bit like two coasts, pasted together."

"Wow, so you'll never be too far away from the beach."

"Yes, but not all the beaches are sandy beaches. On the side that boarders the Atlantic Ocean there are mainly rocks and cliffs. They plunge straight down into the water. The other coast, this one on the Caribbean side, is mostly very shallow and overgrown with mangroves, which are small trees that grow in salt water. They put down roots where the floor is swampy. That's the line between land and water..."

Michael suddenly remembered the image from his history class. He smiled. Now he had an explanation.

"Are there any sandy beaches?" he asked, still thinking about Columbus.

"They have those, too. The bays and inlets mainly consist of miles and miles of beaches. In fact, the bay is where the dolphins lived – they have very fine, white sand. That's where I was heading with your father."

"Was that the same inlet where Christopher Columbus landed all those centuries ago?"

His mother nodded.

"So that's the same spot that Mr. Powell showed to the whole class? And that everyone thought I was wrong about?"

Patricia nodded again and blushed. She felt slightly guilty, but her son didn't notice. He was excited to hear this news. To him, it was just another piece of the puzzle.

Michael wanted to ask more questions, but was suddenly interrupted. A cart, pushed by two flight attendants, had stopped in between the rows of seats. Before he knew what was going on, he was given a food tray.

"Flip down your table so you can put your lunch on it," said Patricia. "Let's take a little break while we eat."

"They couldn't wait until you finished your story?" asked Michael, a little annoyed.

"No, sweetie, my story is way too long. We'll have plenty of time later on. Check out what you got there. Salad? And that stew looks like it's full of carrots and noodles. What do you want to drink? Hurry up, the lady is waiting."

"Can I have a Coke, just this once?"

Michael had seen the bottle on the cart. He was hoping his mom would allow it since this was a special occasion.

"All right, just this once because we're on a plane."

Michael cheered. He was beginning to like flying better by the minute. Especially listening to his mother's fascinating stories. He couldn't wait to hear more.

SIX

Eventually, the flight attendants came by again to take away the food trays. Before they had even passed with their cart, Michael fired off another question.

"So how did you get to Columbus's beach anyway?"

"Well, your father wanted to have all the equipment down by the dolphin bay before dark. It wasn't easy, but he managed to get a hold of a truck after we arrived on Long Island. About an hour before sunset, we reached the bay. We put up our tent, right there by the water."

"You could just do that?"

"Nobody lived around there. But when the truck driver left, he told us that a large European company recently bought all of the northern part of Long Island. They wanted to develop the area."

"What do you mean?"

"They wanted to build a sort of artificial village. The company had plans to construct streets and roads in the middle of the wild landscape. They also wanted to build a small harbor and an airport. After that, they would construct a power plant, a hotel with a shopping mall, a bank, and a post office. Then, the best parcels of land would be put up for sale for very high prices."

"Who would want to live there?"

"Very wealthy people from the United States and Europe who want homes for vacations or even for retirement — lots of people want to spend their old age in the mild climate."

"What about the Indians who live on the islands? What did they think about all this?"

"The Indians?" Patricia asked, amazed.

"Yes, didn't Columbus say that those islands were inhabited by Indians?"

"That's true, Michael, but a lot has happened on the Bahamas since Columbus arrived. There haven't been any Indians on the islands for a long time. Didn't Mr. Powell mention this?"

The boy shook his head.

"What happened to them?" he asked.

"Well, several years after Columbus's arrival, the Spaniards discovered enormous gold mines on Haiti, an island close by. Because they needed lots of people to exploit those mines, they rounded up all the Indians in the Bahamas and deported them as slaves."

"Were they ever allowed to come back?"

"None of them survived. They all perished from diseases and from the backbreaking work."

"That's horrible," Michael exclaimed. "So who lives in the Bahamas now?"

"Mainly people from Africa. In the eighteenth century, Africans were brought over as slaves to work on the cotton plantations. When they abolished slavery in the eighteen hundreds, all those plantations ceased to exist. But the former slaves stayed, even though they continued to live in poverty even until now. A development would push them out of their homes."

Michael kept silent for a while. In less than an hour, he had learned a lot about the Bahamas. Until Mr. Powell's history class on Columbus, he hadn't even known they existed. It was a completely different world than the one he knew. But the puzzle was slowly coming together. Somehow, he was connected to this faraway world.

"What happened after you put up your tent?" Michael was eager to hear the rest of his mother's tale.

"The next morning the dolphins woke us up. We heard them chattering and playing in the water. Your dad couldn't stay away from them. He was in the water with the dolphins in no time. I went in after him.

The dolphins let us play with them and even touch them. Your father even held a dolphin by its fin and let himself be pulled under water. He was an excellent diver. In his spare time he was scuba diving instructor."

"What about you?"

"When I arrived at the island, I'd never been scuba diving, but your dad gave me my first lesson that same day."

"Was it hard?"

"It was a lot easier than I thought it would be. I could handle the equipment pretty well, and breathing under water was almost as effortless as it is on land. It took me less than a week to learn enough to help study the dolphins under water with your father."

"What kind of things did you do?"

"Our first task was to learn how to recognize each animal. There was a group of fourteen dolphins. We had to take pictures of each animal in and out of the water; that was your father's job. I made notes of the external characteristics of each animal: its gender, its size, and likely age, differences in shape and color, and possible scars – especially ones on their dorsal fins. As soon as we were able to distinguish one animal from the next, we gave them names. The first dolphin we named was Gipsy. It was a female who was pregnant at the time. Your father estimated she was seven years old. Aside from her fat belly, you could also easily recognize her by a scar under her one of her eyes."

Michael interrupted her.

"Mom, is it possible that I ever saw this dolphin up close?"

This almost brought tears to Patricia's eyes.

"Of course!" she cried out. "She was your favorite dolphin. You used to call her Mou-Mou."

Patricia remembered that horrible night back in June when Michael's dream made him cry out for Gipsy. The boy was quiet, but Patricia knew he was remembering his dream too.

31

They sat in silence for a few moments. Finally, Michael spoke.

"And after you named all the dolphins, what did you do?"

Patricia continued, relieved that Michael wasn't going to ask more questions about Gipsy.

"We started with the real scientific observations. Every day, we watched the group as a whole and each individual dolphin for many hours. We had so many questions. When was the group present in the bay? What were their main activities? How did the dolphins behave towards each other? Which ones were the leaders and which ones were the followers? How many different ways did they touch each other? What was their reaction when they encountered another large animal? The list of questions grew longer every day. The longer we lived among the dolphins, the more knowledgeable we became and the more we wanted to know."

"How did you keep track of everything?" Michael asked.

"We both used a waterproof camera and an underwater writing slate. We wrote the names of the dolphins on the slate and left room to make daily notes about the animals' behavior during the under water excursion. Whenever something odd happened, we'd try to take pictures. It was my job to copy our notes onto real paper after each dive. Then we would discuss everything. So every day, we learned a bit more about the habits of these extremely fascinating animals."

Michael listened breathlessly. He was envious of his mom's experience.

"I would have loved to do that," he said.

"I can understand that," said Patricia, "and I expected as much. Here, I've got something else for you."

Patricia pulled a beautiful book on dolphins from her purse. Michael's face lit up. It was much thicker than all the books he'd read in the library. He wanted to open it right away, but even more than that, he wanted to hear the rest of the story.

"How long did you guys study those dolphins?"

Patricia smiled. Michael was always hungry for more details. She gave a little sigh, but kept going.

"It wasn't long before we realized our studies would take much longer than the three months we had initially planned. It seemed like the observations could take years. That's when your father started looking for a house to rent, but he couldn't find anything. Then one day he heard about someone who wanted to sell his house on the Caribbean side of the island not far from the new development site. The owner was a retired Canadian who desperately needed money because he wanted to buy a good piece of land in the new development. Your dad was able to buy his house for next to nothing, with all the furniture in it. From that day on, our life was much more comfortable. And, we could stay as long as we wanted."

"Didn't you want to go back home?"

"No, by then I no longer had contact with my family. Nobody answered my letters. And by then, even after such a short time, your father and I were more than just friends. The only thing that could threaten our work was the development. As I told you before, the dolphin bay was within the development site. At the time, we knew very little about their plans. What if they wanted to build a hotel?"

Just thinking about it gave Michael goose bumps.

"Fortunately, the developers arrived at the island around mid-November. They showed their plans to your father and he was very relieved. They didn't have plans for the area by the inlet. But the rest of the land was going to be turned upside down, and quickly. The developers brought a small army of workmen with them. They started tearing through the wilderness with bulldozers, trucks, and cranes. It took less than a month to construct streets and roads. By Christmas, the best parcels of land were already for sale. Luckily, all the activity didn't keep us from our studies – until Christmas, when another spoilsport arrived on the scene."

"Who was that?"

"It was you!"

"Me? How was that possible?"

"Well, we found out I was pregnant on Christmas Day."

"And you thought that was a bad thing?"

"Not exactly. Your father was extremely happy that we were going to have a baby, but it did mean that I wouldn't be able to study the dolphins any more. Pregnant women can't go scuba diving because it can be dangerous for the unborn child and your dad didn't want to take any risks. I was replaced by Jason, a very nice teenager from the island who was going to help us on a regular basis."

"So, you didn't see any dolphins after that, right?"

"Yes, I did. I could still go snorkeling. Later on, I had to go visit them."

"You had to? Did my dad tell you to?"

"No, the doctor said I should."

"The doctor?" asked Michael. "Why?"

"There was a new doctor on Long Island who came just after the developers. He was originally from Africa, but he'd studied medicine in Russia. There, he assisted with the first underwater deliveries in the Western world."

Patricia watched as her son's expression changed.

"Mom," he asked, sitting up straight. "Was I born underwater?"

He looked her directly in the eyes hoping with all his heart to get a positive answer.

"Yes," she replied.

Michael felt blissful.

"Are you happy about that?" Patricia asked, almost moved to tears.

"It's so fantastic!" he cried. "I was born underwater, just like a dolphin!"

If it wasn't for the fact that he was on a plane full of people, Michael would have shouted for joy.

SEVEN

A signal sounded and all the signs in the cabin lit up. Once again, the passengers had to fasten their seatbelts.

"Are we almost there?" Michael asked.

He'd been on this plane for almost two hours. His watch said it was ten minutes to three.

"You'll have to change the time," Patricia said. "It's an hour later in this part of the country. It'll be four in the afternoon when we land in Atlanta. It's going to be a long day."

But Michael wasn't listening.

"Look at all those skyscrapers down there," Michael said excitedly looking out the window.

The plane turned and tilted. Suddenly, Michael could see a spectacular panoramic view of Atlanta.

Five minutes later, the plane made another loop, followed by yet another ten minutes later.

"Why aren't we landing?" Michael asked. "It seems like the plane is going around in circles."

"The pilot is probably waiting for permission to land."

"Why can't he just do it?"

"We have to wait our turn, Michael. There are a lot of planes that want to land in Atlanta."

Finally, the turns stopped and Michael noticed the ground getting closer and closer. Suddenly, he heard a strange noise coming from underneath the plane.

"What was that?" he asked, startled.

"Don't worry Michael. That's just the landing gear coming down. During the flight, the wheels are pulled up inside."

After that, it went very quickly. The houses and cars that looked like toys at first grew bigger by the second. The plane flew over a large enclosure, and then Michael saw the plane's gigantic shadow on the ground. They touched down. The bulky jet wobbled a few times, as if it had to keep its balance, and then it put on the brakes.

What an adventure, Michael thought, and started applauding with some of the other passengers. Flying was a lot more fun that he had thought it would be. He was already looking forward to his next flight.

But that could be a while. The plane had arrived in Atlanta, but because of the earlier delay Patricia was concerned that they might have missed their connection to the Bahamas. She'd already realized this before they took off in Chicago. Fortunately, there were more flights to Nassau today. She hoped one of those planes would have two empty seats …

The plane came to a stop. The passengers got up and stood in a line until they could leave the aircraft through a long sleeve. They walked past corridors and stairs like a flock of sheep. Then they had to line up for some kind of checkpoint. Once again Michael's patience was put to the test.

"Are we going to the next plane?" Michael asked when they were finally through the line. Even though it was only 4:30, the boy was starting to feel tired. After all, his day had started almost twelve hours earlier, and all this sitting and waiting around turned out to be much more exhausting than he ever would have thought.

"First we have to pick up our luggage," Patricia said. "Then we'll go to the international terminal, where we'll see if there are seats on one of the later flights. We may have to stay here for a couple of hours."

Michael gasped. He liked traveling, but enough was enough.

They'd waited too much, as far as Michael was concerned. After they collected their luggage, and waited on another line for what seemed like forever, it finally was their turn.

"We're lucky!" Patricia exclaimed after she finished talking to the flight attendant at the counter.

"We're lucky?" Michael asked.

"We just got the last two seats. Come on, give me the suitcases. Let's go to the gate."

Michael cheered. They would be airborne in less than two hours. He felt like he was waking up. He badly wanted to see the Bahamas, and now it was practically within his reach. The place where he was born under water. And now, more than ever, Michael wanted to learn the whole story about his birth. After re-checking their luggage and having their passports inspected, Patricia found a quiet little corner, where she would tell Michael the best part of her tale.

"Finally," said Michael, after they had settled into a pair of chairs in the waiting lounge, "because I really want to know how I was born under water. How come you guys did that?"

"I told you about the doctor from Africa," Patricia said. "He grew up in a tribe where babies have been born under water since ancient times. He was the son of the tribal chief, which gave him the chance to go away to school. Going to college is not all that common in all countries. Later, he got permission to finish his medical studies in Russia. He participated in a big research project studying underwater deliveries by the Black Sea, which is a big inland sea in Europe. With some of the deliveries, they even had a dolphin present. Those births went even more smoothly. As soon as the doctor received his degree, he wanted to practice medicine in a location where there were dolphins. He really wanted to keep working with those animals."

"That doctor must have been really happy when he met you two," Michael remarked.

"You got that right! And of course your father was excited about the idea right from the start."

"How about you? Did you also want to have your baby underwater?

"Me?" Patricia asked. "I wasn't exactly jumping up and down. I didn't want to be a guinea pig. I was really scared it might be dangerous."

"But Mom, everything turned out great. If you had asked me then, I would have wanted it too."

"I don't doubt that." Patricia chuckled. "You're just like your dad."

Michael beamed; this was the first time his mom had ever said that he took after his father. He was beginning to like the man better and better.

Patricia continued.

"In the end," she said, "the doctor managed to convince me to do it. He proved there were hardly any risks involved. One thing he told me was that an unborn baby is really a little underwater animal. In that way, it's very similar to a dolphin. He also told me that an underwater birth has a number of benefits for the baby. The whole delivery happens much more smoothly and quietly. Compared to a regular birth, it's almost a pleasant experience for the child. And since the transition into the outside world occurs so gradually, there is a lot less stress to the baby's brain. A baby's memory supposedly starts functioning much earlier when it's born underwater."

Michael had to agree with his mother. That would explain why it was so easy for him to remember things that happened ages ago. On the other hand, that wasn't quite true for everything!

"And then, of course, there were these dolphins."

"Yeah, that's right," Michael exclaimed. "So what exactly was their job during the birth?"

Patricia smiled.

"You see," she said, "the doctor was convinced and your father was of the same opinion, that it would be very easy for a dolphin to communicate with an unborn baby. After all, dolphins are highly intelligent animals and they have remarkable senses. Through these sense, the doctor and your father thought that the dolphins would be able to give certain signals that could have a positive effect on the birthing process."

"That's amazing," Michael said, "but … is that really true?"

Again Patricia smiled.

"I had a hard time believing it at first, but it wasn't long before I started noticing it myself."

"Really?"

"Sure! After all, the doctor had advised me to swim as often as possible. He also wanted me to do lots of breathing exercises under water. Your dad and I used to do that together in the shallow waters of Mangrove Bay, which was not far from where we lived. Each time I went into the water, dolphin Gipsy would join me."

"Mou-Mou!" Michael cried out.

"She was pregnant too. She often touched her belly to mine. When our two little ones were so close together, it was as if they were communicating. And after Derby, her baby, was born, he and Gipsy would swim up to me and touch my belly with their pointy snouts. First, I would feel their vibrations, and then I would feel you moving inside me. Clearly there was a kind of communication between you and them."

"Awesome!"

"Absolutely. From that moment on, I had complete faith in the dolphins. With so many assistants, how could this delivery go wrong? But then, suddenly, the developers threatened their existence."

"What happened?"

"In the beginning of June, the development project got a new manager. The first thing he did was consider building the Hotel Columbus in a completely different location."

"At the site of the dolphin inlet?" Michael was shocked.

"Oh yes, because that creep thought of the dolphins as entertainment that would attract many, many tourists."

"What a jerk. How dare he? Didn't my dad go against him?"

"Are you kidding? Of course! He was just like you. As soon as he heard about their plans, he went after them. He threatened to take action and go to the Bahamian authorities. His reaction scared them. Dolphins are a protected species. The day after, they promised to cancel their plans, so it looked as if they would leave your father and his animals alone."

"Phew!" Michael let out a sigh.

"In the meantime, they were building one villa after another. In the spring, they finished the power plant, and by the summer, the small harbor was done. Then they started work on the airport, but they stopped working during the hottest months. By the time the rainy season started in August, most of the white inhabitants had already left the island. And precisely during that humid period, you announced yourself."

"Ah," Michael cried, "now it's getting exciting!"

Patricia laughed, then continued her story.

"Yes, indeed, on August 21st it happened. Your father had left early that morning. He didn't go scuba diving in case I needed to reach him. You were supposed to be born any minute. Your dad was only gone a few hours when I felt wetness trickling down my legs. My water broke. I called the doctor on the radio right away. I also asked anyone who was listening on the same wavelength, if they could notify your father. Less than fifteen minutes later, I saw the doctor's car coming. He said we should go to Mangrove Bay together. At that time of the year, the temperature of the water in the shallow inlet was over ninety degrees. At first, I wanted to wait for your father to return, but the doctor said it would be better for me to be in that warm water. Ten minutes later, we got to the bay. I had to wade in a little bit until the water was about two and half feet deep. The doctor had changed into his swimming shorts and followed me into the water. There he told me to lower myself into the warm water. It felt divine; I could feel you were enjoying it too."

Patricia stopped for a second. She saw that Michael was listening with his eyes closed.

"And then what happened?" he asked.

"Well, then, just when I started wondering where those dolphins were, I saw a line of triangular fins speeding toward us from the ocean. I knew those shapes too well to be afraid. The whole group of dolphins swam close. Most of them kept a respectful distance, as if they were aware of the gravity of the situation. Only a single animal approached me. That was Gipsy. The contractions began as soon as she arrived at my side. I used the breathing techniques I'd practiced with your father. They helped, because during that first wave of labor pains, I hardly felt anything. I was encouraged, but I knew it was only the beginning. The waves of pain gradually got stronger. Luckily, there was some time to rest in between the contractions. But those breaks got shorter and shorter. At some point, I started to wonder what was taking your father so long. He would have so loved to be there. The doctor tried to reassure me. And then I noticed that Derby, Gipsy's young one, wasn't there either. Normally, he was always next to his mother. Where could that little dolphin be? But I didn't have much time to worry about it. The contractions started up again. And then ..."

Patricia hesitated.

"Yes, and then?" Michael asked, opening his eyes.

"And then ... you were born."

Upon hearing those words, Michael grinned from ear to ear.

Her son looked deliriously happy, so Patricia ended her story there.

Was it really necessary to tell him everything? Should he know that just before he was born, things almost went very wrong? Should he know that he had suddenly started to move wildly, as if he wanted to get away? That he had twisted and turned the wrong way and couldn't be born normally? That the doctor almost panicked? That just in time, Gipsy came to the rescue? She touched Patricia's big belly with her snout as if she wanted to whisper something to little Michael. Then the baby started moving again and turned around just in time to come into the world a perfectly healthy baby. First in the world of water, then in the world of air. The doctor was completely surprised.

No, it wasn't necessary to tell him all of that, or to tell him how hard he had cried after he was born. Patricia remembered how little Derby came swimming up, terribly upset. It was as if the tiny dolphin knew why this human baby was crying so hard. No, Michael didn't need to know that either. And for a while longer, Patricia would keep silent about the body that washed ashore that same evening. Unless the past caught up with them faster than she expected ...

EIGHT

Monday, August 3, Nassau harbor

It was already dark, but the *Day Queen* still hadn't left. Michael and his mom had climbed aboard earlier in the afternoon, along with six other passengers. Patricia's plan was to travel to Long Island on that old mail boat like she'd done during her first trip to the island.

At first, everything worked out perfectly. They'd arrived in the Bahamas late the night before and stayed in a small hotel on the outskirts of Nassau. In the morning, Patricia had had no trouble securing two fares on the small boat. That's when things went wrong.

Normally the ship sailed at two in the afternoon. All the goods had arrived. They were piled in the hold or were stacked on deck where they were roped up securely.

A few times, Patricia asked the captain when they would be leaving. But the man hardly responded. He only said, "We'll see."

His attitude didn't surprise Patricia. Not only was she a woman, she was also just a passenger. The captain thought he was superior. The way he saw it, he didn't even need passengers. He already made a nice profit from shipping the goods. He felt that the passengers ought to be grateful that he even allowed them on board. Michael thought he was completely outrageous.

"Why is everything so slow out here?" he asked his mom. "Can't these people do anything the regular way?"

"What do you mean by 'regular?'" Patricia asked. "Our way of life? I don't think the Bahamians would want to live the way we do. They think that in our country, everyone is rushed. You know how many people have heart attacks because of stress in the United Sates? We can't demand that these people adopt our lifestyle in their own country. And working in a tropical climate with no air conditioning is a lot harder. You'll feel it yourself in the next couple of days."

None of that had occurred to Michael.

"Even so, Mom, we'll lose time because we have to wait. If we had known that the ship would leave so much later, we could have visited Nassau. Now we have to spend the whole afternoon on this tub."

Patricia smiled.

"Michael," she said, "have you ever thought about the fact that you can look at something other than monuments in a foreign country?"

The boy frowned.

"Like what?"

"The people around you, for starters. You can learn a lot from their way of working, gesturing, talking, and dealing with one another. When you travel to a different country, you don't need to limit yourself to the tourist spots. Connecting with the local population will help you get to know the country. I learned that from your father."

Michael kept quiet. And then he smiled.

"Ok, Mom, but what if the people around you disappear all of a sudden?"

Patricia hadn't noticed that all passengers were going ashore and leaving.

"I'm afraid," she said dryly, "we won't be sailing tonight."

She turned to a Bahamian who was about to step onto the gangplank. The man told her that the special cargo the captain had been waiting for all day wouldn't be arriving until the next morning. The ship wouldn't be leaving until seven the following day. Patricia immediately marched up to the galley, where cook confirmed the story: they would be in the harbor all night. They could spend the night on board, if they wished. But he would be the only other person on the ship.

Patricia didn't have much of a choice. The cost of two taxi rides plus a double room in a hotel was triple the amount of their boat trip to the island. She absolutely had to avoid unexpected expenses. They would have to spend the night on board the ship.

Although he ship was moored in the middle of the harbor by the bridge to the luxurious Paradise Island, the whole neighborhood looked decidedly dark and gloomy. There was nowhere to get anything to eat or drink.

"We'll just have to go to bed hungry and thirsty," Patricia resolved. "We've already finished our food supply for this afternoon. And we won't get any meals until the ship sails. Sorry, Michael."

Patricia led Michael to their cabin. The cabin they were given was located at the other side of the corridor from the one she'd stayed in during her first trip on the *Day Queen*, some fourteen years ago. A little after eight, they were both in their bunks.

The hours passed slowly. The harbor district quieted down. Sometimes speeding cars would disturb the still night, rounding corners with screeching tires.

By one in the morning, neither Patricia nor Michael had slept a wink. Inside the closed-up ship, it was steaming hot. The cook was snoring, heavily on a couch in the dining hall. He'd locked all the doors and windows so nobody could enter the ship.

Suddenly, a car came around the corner, but instead of accelerating it slowed down. Then it came to a halt alongside the ship. Six men got out of the vehicle and jumped aboard. They knocked on the windows with a heavy metal object. They shouted for someone to open up. The cook jumped up immediately. He ran to the door and opened it a little bit. Through the crack, he yelled for the men to leave. He said he was the only one on board. But, unfortunately, at just the wrong moment, Patricia appeared. The men outside saw her right away.

Now they started kicking and pushing the door. A white woman meant money, and that's what they were after.

The cook was vastly outnumbered. He didn't stand a chance against the robbers. Finally, the men pushed through the door.

"This lady is not your ordinary white woman," the cook shouted at them. "She used to live here a long time ago. Now she's coming back to the island," he said just before he was pushed aside roughly by the gang leader.

The gang leader stood directly in front of Patricia, towering over her. She blocked the entrance to the cabin where Michael was lying quietly in his bunk.

"What are you doing going to Long Island?" he asked, towering above her.

"Visiting my husband's grave," she answered.

"You're lying," he shouted. "You're just trying to fool us."

"That's not true," Patricia cried out. "My husband is buried under the lighthouse at Cape Santa Maria."

"That's the haunted lighthouse," a man from the back of the group said. The gang leader turned abruptly.

"What do you know about that?" he asked.

"I know all about it," the man called, "because I'm from Long Island."

"So get up here!" the leader bellowed.

A little shuffling took place and a young guy slowly came closer.

"Yeah, that's right," he said. "I recognize her. She's Ben Jansen's wife – he's the man buried in the haunted lighthouse."

"Are you sure?"

"Absolutely," the man said, getting really excited.

"Then we'd better leave," the gang leader concluded.

He didn't say another word. As fast as they had come, the harbor pirates took off.

While locking the door again, the cook apologized for not coming to Patricia's aid. After what he had just learned, he had a newfound respect for her.

Michael had heard everything, too. Patricia knew her son would demand an explanation. In spite of the late hour, she decided to give it to him.

"Michael," she said, her voice trembling, "when we were on the plane, I told you the whole story up to your birth. You were so happy, I decided to stop right there. I wanted to wait until we were on the island. But the past, once again, caught up with us before I was ready. And yes, as you just heard, your father died. It happened the same day you were born. He was buried the next day in a lighthouse that was under construction. But, I don't know anything about the ghost story those guys were talking about. Tomorrow, on our trip, I'll tell you all the details. You've had enough excitement for one night."

NINE

The sun was shining when the *Day Queen* left Nassau harbor and headed south. The Caribbean was quiet. Patricia and Michael stood by the bow, watching. Now, on the last leg of their journey, Patricia knew she had to tell her son the hardest part of her narrative.

"After you were born," Patricia began, "I left Mangrove Bay in a state of extreme happiness. The doctor took me home. All I could think about was holding you in my arms there. When we got home, I realized that I had forgotten about your dad. Immediately, I saw the note I left for him, untouched. I waited impatiently for him to come home.

"In the meantime, all of the island people heard you were born. By the time it started to get dark, I was really worried. I knew something had happened. Finally, at nine o'clock, a car stopped in front of the door. Four men got out. They came inside, but none of them would look me in the eye. I was afraid the worst had happened. Indeed, earlier in the evening they'd found your father's body on the beach. He was wearing all his diving gear. He'd gone diving, even though I had specifically asked him not to. Suddenly, I didn't know how I felt. The enormous joy of your birth was followed by a deep sadness; I had gained someone, but someone else was taken from me. Fortunately, the doctor gave me some medicine to help me calm down. A short while later, I fell asleep, which was good because I really needed it."

"What did they do with Dad?"

"The next morning a lot of people came to our house. I wanted to see your father one last time. But I couldn't; he was already in his coffin." Patricia looked out across the water.

"That was so fast," Michael said, shaking his head.

"Yes, Michael, because of the tropical heat, a body starts to decompose very quickly out here. Usually, they bury someone who dies the same day, or the next at the latest. They asked me if they should organize a memorial service. I didn't know what to tell them. I never talked about any of these things with your father. The only thing I remembered was a conversation we had about lighthouse-keepers since there were plans to build a lighthouse at Cape Santa Maria as well. When we heard about that, your father told me he would love to be lighthouse-keeper in his old age. That way he could live near the ocean and write a couple of books without any distraction. Just thinking about it made him happy. A few days before he died, they began laying the foundations for that tower. I asked Mr. Braunschwein, one of the developers, if he would have any objections to burying your father in that tower. He thought that was a great idea, that it would be a monument worthy of someone who had always loved the ocean. Your father was buried there. A large number of the local island dwellers attended because your dad was well loved among them."

For a few moments, they stood in silence listening to the sound of boat cutting through the waves.

"And what about that ghost story? Is any of that true?" Michael asked, finally.

"As I said last night, Michael, I don't know anything about that. But I can imagine how such a story could spring to life. The Bahamians are very superstitious. They fear corpses and the dead. Wild horses couldn't drag them to a graveyard at night. They think that ghosts and spirits come out at night. And perhaps because someone is buried in that lighthouse, they made it into a ghost tower. Which is ridiculous because your father lies buried under ten feet of concrete, at least."

"What happened to us after that?"

"Some of the local girls helped take care of you, which allowed me some time to organize things. There's a lot of work to do when someone dies. At that time, I didn't have any financial problems. Your father had a big bank account, and we owned the house. So I didn't need to worry about that. But I started looking for a job anyway. I didn't want to spend his money right away. I knew they needed teachers on the island. I thought I would certainly be considered."

"So things worked out better than you thought."

"At first they did. But eventually things got much harder. There was an important document that I couldn't find. When I was a few weeks pregnant, I asked your father to acknowledge you as his child in writing. You never knew what could happen. At first, he laughed at me, but when he realized I was serious, he did it. I watched him write and sign the statement, but, unfortunately, I didn't put the document away myself. After the funeral I searched all our papers. For days, I practically turned the house upside down, but it was all for nothing. The fact that I couldn't find the document was devastating. It was the only proof he was your father. Don't forget, we weren't married."

"Why was that so terrible?" Michael asked. "He was dead anyway!"

"That's true, but it meant you couldn't have his last name."

"How come you guys never got married?"

"We wanted to as soon as I got pregnant, but we needed to have the right papers. I wrote to Boston more than once in order to get them, but nobody in my family was willing to help, so we postponed getting married until we went back to the States."

"But I still don't get why that's so bad. I don't care if I have your last name or his."

"Yes, of course, Michael, you're right. It's not a big deal; it's that you couldn't inherit anything from him without his acknowledging you."

"Was my dad that rich?"

"Pretty rich. Six months before we left for the Bahamas, his mother died. His parents left a fortune and your father was the only heir. It was because of his inheritance that he could afford his expeditions and our stay in the Bahamas, otherwise it wouldn't have been possible. And because of it, he was able to buy the house on Long Island."

"So who inherited this fortune?" Michael asked, watching a pair of seagulls flying over the *Day Queen*. There was something – a fish, most likely – splashing in the water to the right of the boat.

"It went to a distant cousin of your father's. She was the only heir who was left. When they learned of his death in the States, the estate lawyer granted her all of the twelve houses he owned."

"Too bad," said Michael, "but out here something was left over, right?"

"True, but regrettably that didn't last long. This cousin wasn't satisfied with what she had. She demanded I move out of the house in the Bahamas and put the money in her bank account. But I refused."

"Good for you, Mom!"

"She didn't give up though. From California, she tried for years to get me out of the house. After almost three years, she finally got her way."

"How come?"

"A Bahamian court ruled in her favor. The bank account was frozen and the police escorted me out of the house. This was over ten years ago."

"What did you do?"

"As if I hadn't already had my share of bad luck, shortly thereafter, they told me that they couldn't renew my teaching contract for the next school year. Since I didn't have an income, I had no other choice but to return to Boston with you. I knew I couldn't come knocking on your grandpa's – my father's – door. Not only had I left for the Bahamas against his wishes, I had returned an unwed, single mother.

When I arrived in Boston, he didn't even want to see me. My mother wanted to help, but she didn't have the heart to go against my father's wishes. I looked for a job in my old hometown, but I couldn't find anything. Unemployment was rampant at the time and as a single mother, I didn't encounter a whole lot of support. Only a few people even considered me for an interesting job. But because of my father's meddling, the opportunities always fizzled out. After a year of struggling, I realized I needed to radically break with my past. From that moment on, I wanted to forget everything that had happened in the Bahamas as quickly as possible. And, I didn't want anything to do with my family any longer. I decided to move to a very different city. I thought Madison, Wisconsin was the perfect place for me to start a whole new life. I made sure that nobody ever found out about my past. That's also the reason why I didn't want to tell you anything. Can you understand that?" Patricia turned so that she was leaning against the railing. She looked down at her son.

Michael nodded.

"But then why did you decide to take this trip? You could have told me all of this at home."

"Certainly, Michael. Even though I've told you about a lot of things, you still don't know the whole story. As far as the rest is concerned, you'll discover that for yourself on the island. As for me, I still have so many unanswered questions, but maybe we'll find the answers together. Who knows?"

TEN

Wednesday, August 5

For the first time in ten years, Michael saw the island where he was born. He didn't recognize the area where the *Day Queen* docked, but as soon as he was in the Land Rover on the highway heading north, Michael saw dozens of familiar scenes out the window. All these years they were stored deep in his memory waiting to be released. At one moment, he knew with unexpected certainty that there would be a large bay just past the next curve in the road. And it turned out he was right! Michael wondered how this was possible, but he hesitated before saying anything to his mother. After all, they had only just met the Rogers.

When the Rogers family saw Michael and his mother on the pier, dragging their suitcases, they immediately offered to help. They seemed very friendly. They were from Canada, and both Mr. and Mrs. Rogers were teachers at the new high school on Long Island. The *Day Queen* was supposed to be bringing something they'd mail-ordered, but when they arrived, their package wasn't on board the ship. They insisted on giving Michael and Patricia a ride, since it turned out the Rogers lived very close to the place Patricia and her son were staying.

"It must be quite a thrill," Mrs. Rogers said in a shrill voice, "to be back on the island again after such a long time."

"It certainly is. I can't wait to see how the house looks," Patricia said.

"Don't get your hopes up," Mrs. Rogers said. "It's been in bad shape for years. The garden is a real jungle. And I'm sure everything inside is covered in dust. But I'll be happy to help you clean her up."

"Thank you very much," Patricia said. "That's very kind of you."

The house made Patricia think of Ben's cousin. That nasty woman had some nerve. First, she'd done everything in her power to push Patricia out of the house, and then she just left it empty and abandoned it.

Still, Patricia wasn't unhappy with the current situation. She'd taken a set of extra keys with her when she left, as a souvenir. Now they would certainly come in handy. Before the cousin could learn that they'd stayed at the house unlawfully, Patricia and Michael would be back in the States.

Suddenly, the Land Rover slowed down. Mr. Rogers turned left. Patricia could tell by the weeds on the road that few cars ever passed by.

"Just a few more minutes and we're there," Mr. Rogers said. These were the first words he'd spoken since he started driving Land Rover. Mrs. Rogers had more than made up for his silence. The car came to a stop right by the driveway.

"Go on and open the door," Mrs. Rogers said cheerfully. "We'll grab your suitcases."

As Patricia walked to the front door with her keys, she hoped the lock hadn't been changed. It was her lucky day; she sighed as the front door opened without any trouble. Inside, the house smelled very musty and it was pitch black. The storm fence in front of the windows blocked any light.

"Let's get rid of this fence," Mrs. Rogers called. "Come on, Ted, give me a hand. This is no job for a woman to do on her own."

She turned to Patricia.

"Open the windows and get some air in there."

Within an hour the house was slightly more livable. Gas and electricity were turned on, and theyd put clean sheets on two beds.

"Much better," said Mrs. Rogers, nodding. "As soon as we get home, I'll send our son Johnny over with some food, so you two won't starve tonight and tomorrow. Johnny will be so happy to meet Michael. I think they'll like each other. And, in the morning I'll be back with brooms and cleaning supplies. By tomorrow night you won't even recognize the place."

"Thanks for all your help, Mr. and Mrs. Rogers," Patricia said, placing a hand on Michael's shoulders as they watched their new friends climb into their Land Rover.

"Oh, please, from now on, we're Ted and Jane," Mrs. Rogers said waving at them through the window. Then Mr. Rogers – Ted – started the Land Rover and drove off slowly.

There they were, mother and son in the house they had been forced to leave ten years ago. Although Jane came across as rather pushy, Patricia was happy to have someone to help her on the island. She wondered how many of her old friends still lived here on Long Island. Tomorrow, when Jane was here, she'd probably hear a lot of stories and have the chance to ask some questions. And, she was glad Michael would have a friend out here to help make his trip more fun. She was curious to meet this Johnny.

ELEVEN

Thursday, August 6

"This is the best view of the whole development," Johnny said from the top of the hill.

Michael trailed a few feet behind Johnny, having some trouble climbing the last few steps. He wasn't used to this muggy weather. His forehead dripped with sweat and his t-shirt was soaked.

Finally, Michael caught up. He quickly moved into the shade of the small pavilion.

Indeed, the view was worth the trouble. Johnny, who was a year older than Michael and had been living on the island for years, was happy to play tour guide.

"Now we're looking north," he said. "The Atlantic is over there on your right. It's dark blue where it gets deep. Also, there are always waves out there because the wind usually blows in from that direction. The Caribbean is on the other side of the island. It's light blue, and most of the time it's really still. To the left of the main island is a smaller one called Hog Island. Can you see the airport and the marina?"

"What's a marina?" Michael asked.

"That's a small harbor. You don't know that?"

Michael shook his head.

"Well, it has room for about a dozen small ships to moor. You can easily recognize this marina by the two little lighthouses down there. They mark the entrance."

"Is one of them the haunted tower?"

"Oh no!" Johnny exclaimed. "That's all the way on the other side of the development. You can hardly see it from here. Look, all the way out there by the Atlantic coast. See that white little hat sticking out from the green? That's the top of it."

Michael looked in that direction for a minute.

"Johnny, do you believe the ghost stories about the tower?" he asked abruptly.

"Where did you hear that?" Johnny called out.

"Well, you know. On the boat I overheard something ..."

"Honestly, I don't know. My parents say it's totally untrue, but a lot of the locals really believe in it. When it's dark out, they won't go anywhere near it, not for all the money in the world. Some people say that sometimes there's a spooky light around the tower."

"I'm sure there is," Michael called. "I mean, it's a lighthouse!"

"No, it's not, actually. That lighthouse never really worked."

"That's so weird. Do you think we can go and take a look up close?"

"Sure, I don't mind ... as long as it's during the day."

"You're not scared are you?"

"No, but I'd rather not seek out creepy places like that at night."

"Are there more haunted places on the island?" Michael asked curiously.

"More than I'd like," said Johnny. "There are some dark caves pretty close by, a few scary ruins, and a whole lot of mysterious blue holes."

"Wow, that sounds awesome," Michael yelled. "When are we going?"

"You like scary places?"

"Absolutely," Michael answered.

"Okay," Johnny said, walking down the stairs. "The Great Cave isn't too far from here. Come on."

At the bottom of the stairs, the two boys climbed on their bikes. A short while later, Johnny stopped at a side-path.

"We'll have to walk from here, the road slopes down too steeply."

The path was well kept. It was too neat for Michael's taste. At the bottom was a cave so big that a truck could have easily driven through the entrance. But what he saw disappointed him.

"Who put up all these stone tables?" he asked.

"The hotel people," said Johnny. "They organize parties here every week. I've been a couple of times with my parents. They burn torches to light the cave, and there's a live band playing in that corner over there. It's fun!"

"They should have left it the way it was. How many bats did they have to chase away for this?"

"There's more than enough space for those animals in the other caves," said Johnny. "The bottom of this island is like one big hunk of Swiss cheese. Come on, I'll show you a blue hole; you're going to love it."

"Is that a cave too?"

"Yes, but one that filled up with water."

It took a couple of minutes to climb the hill to their bikes. Michael felt sweat trickling down his back

"Johnny! Not so fast," he called down the road as Johnny zoomed off. "I'm not used to the weather out here yet." The air was thick and humid; Michael could hardly breathe.

Suddenly, Johnny slammed on the brakes.

"Look," he yelled, "that's a blue hole."

Off to the left was a perfectly round lake. Michael estimated it was about a hundred yards across.

"How deep is it?" Michael asked, hopping off his bike.

"No one knows for sure. Some people say it's hundreds of feet deep and that it runs underground for miles, maybe as far as the ocean."

"Does anybody ever just dive in?"

"As far as I know, nobody does, and I don't think you'll ever find a volunteer. People are scared of getting sucked under, or caught by some kind of monster."

"Wow," Michael exclaimed.

"Can you drink the water from the blue holes?"

"No, it's too salty. But, if you're thirsty, I have a better solution. Come on."

For the umpteenth time that day, Michael jumped on his bike. They rode down the street on the left side with the other traffic. The Bahamas used to be a British colony, so everyone drove on the opposite side of what Michael was used to in the States. He liked that every driver they passed raised a hand to greet them.

"And now we'll have a feast." Johnny said, climbing off his bike and leaning it against a fence.

Then, he opened a gate and led Michael into the yard.

"Who are we visiting?" Michael asked.

"This is Stemman's house. He's German. But he's not here right now. He only lives here from Christmas until Easter when the weather is nice and cool."

"So why are we here?"

"Weren't you thirsty? He has some juicy mango's hanging here. We'll go pick them."

"Is that allowed?"

"Would you rather let them spoil on the trees? Since Stemman's not home, we might as well enjoy them."

The mango looked like a small melon. Michael peeled it and bit into the juicy fruit.

"It's good, isn't it?" Johnny asked.

"Yes, and it's so beautiful up here. What a great view of the Atlantic!"

"Yeah, but be careful at the end of the garden. There's a ravine there."

"Still, I wouldn't mind staying in this house."

"Me either. This is one of the most expensive places in the development."

"But they only live here for a couple of months a year?"

"Yes," said Johnny, "Mr. Stemman is a German industrialist. He is filthy rich, but he can't ever stay here for long periods of time. The same with Mr. Wagner."

Johnny pointed in the direction of the house next door. Michael spotted a series of odd panels on the roof. He pointed them out to Johnny.

"What are those things?"

"Those are solar panels. Mr. Wagner had them installed a few years back. He gets all of his electricity from them."

"Doesn't the island have an electric company?"

"Yes, but Mr. Wagner once had a dispute about his bill. When they shut off his electricity, he was angry and left for Miami. Two days later he came back with a whole bunch of batteries and these solar panels, so they could keep their electricity."

"Who are 'they?'"

"The managers of the development and of the Hotel Columbus, a Swiss called Braunschwein, and an American called Dulles. I'm sure you'll get to know them while you're here. I don't like them. All they want is money. That's the only time they act friendly. Come on, I'll show you the hotel."

The boys had just gotten on their bikes, when a white mini-van coming from the opposite direction stopped in front of them. A muscular man with gray hair was behind the wheel.

"That's Roby. He's the nicest American on the entire island. I'll introduce you," Johnny said.

Meanwhile, the elderly man stepped out of the car.

"Hi there, Johnny!" he called.

"Hello, Roby. How are you? This is Michael."

"Michael?" Roby exclaimed. "I think I know Michael from way back."

"Really?" Michael asked.

"I knew you when you were only this big." Roby reached down until his hand was level with his knee.

"But now you're a big boy. And you look exactly like your dad."

"Did you know my father?" Michael was suddenly very excited.

"Not all that well, but enough to be able to see him in you."

"Can you tell me anything about him?"

"Certainly, but you'll have to stop by and see me another time. This morning I heard you and your mother were back on the island. Tell her hello and that I said you're both welcome in our home anytime. Unfortunately, I have to go now. See you soon!"

Roby waved, walked back to his mini-van, and drove off.

"He's a great guy," said Johnny. "You can ask him anything, and he always has an answer."

"What kind of work does he do?"

"He used to be a helicopter pilot in the army, but you'd never think he was a soldier. He's really friendly. You'll see for yourself how different the hotel guys are. Come on, let's get going."

The road started to drop. Here the road wasn't very hilly. In the distance, Michael saw the dolphin bay and the tiny island. By now it was practically a familiar sight. Michael thought of Mr. Powell showing the class that satellite photo. He was very curious to see if that little bridge was really there.

Again, he thought back to what his mom had told him on the plane. Precisely because he was born under water, he was able to remember places and events from his earliest years much better than other people could.

The two boys came to a rectangular mangrove swamp. Across the narrowest part and not far from the large inlet, there was a small, concrete bridge. When they walked over it, Johnny couldn't understand why Michael looked so smug. After walking a bit further, they stopped.

"Look, Michael," Johnny said ceremoniously, "now I will show you a very important historic location. You'll never guess who once set foot on this island."

"Really? What if I do?"

"I'll treat you to a lemonade in the bar of the hotel over there."

"All right, Johnny, get out your allowance because on Wednesday, October 17, 1492, after first reaching the islands of San Salvador and Santa Maria, here landed none other than the bold navigator and the discoverer of the New World, Mr. Christopher Columbus." Michael took a bow. "Hurry up, Johnny, let's get to that hotel bar, 'cause I'm thirsty."

Johnny stared at Michael, wide-eyed.

"Where did you learn that?"

"Well, in school, of course. Where else would I have learned that? Come on, Johnny, our lemonade is getting warm."

The Hotel Columbus was on a beautiful sandy beach at the far end of the bay. It was three stories high. The walls were whitewashed and all the woodwork was stained a dark brown. On the beach, they'd put up beach umbrellas to protect the tourists from the glare of the sun. Although, there weren't many guests left at this time of the year. The hotel bar was practically empty.

Johnny ordered two bottles of lemonade and brought them out to the terrace, where Michael was sitting at a table in the shade.

"Johnny, did you know there used to be dolphins living in this bay?"

"Yes, I've heard about them."

"My father was the first to come and study them, together with my mother. This hotel wasn't here yet. After my father died, they built it."

"Isn't your father buried under the Cape Santa Maria lighthouse?"

"Exactly. He died in a stupid diving accident. If he hadn't, the hotel would never have been built here and we would still be able to play with the dolphins. They should throw the boss of this dump to the sharks."

"Be quiet, Michael," Johnny said. "Here he comes."

A pick-up truck came to a halt in front of the hotel. A plump man in his forties got out. His face had sharp features and his hair was slicked back. He was wearing sporty clothes: orange Bermuda shorts and a t-shirt with the name of the hotel written across his chest. Without so much as a glance at the boys, he walked past them and into the hotel.

"Too bad he was gone so fast," Michael said. "I should have given him a piece of my mind about chasing away the dolphins."

"Take it easy, Michael, the man owns everything around here. You'd better stay on his good side. He's capable of shutting down your electricity, just like that. Then you can't do anything here."

"Okay, I guess you're right. I don't think Mom would like that."

Just as the boys got up, a black man walked in their direction.

"Turn me into a dolphin if that isn't Michael O'Neil," he said, grinning.

"Who are you and how do you know me?" the boy asked, surprised.

"I'm Jason; I used to work with your dad. I just ran into Roby at the marina. He told me you and your mother are back. I'm so happy to see you. You grew up to be a sturdy fellow, didn't you? When can I start teaching you to scuba dive?"

"You'd really do that?"

"Certainly! Your dad taught me, way back when, so I might as well return the favor."

"Tomorrow?" Michael asked, about to burst with excitement.

"Wonderful," Jason said, laughing. "It's a date! I'll see tomorrow at eight at the swimming pool by the marina."

"Awesome!" Michael yelled.

He would never have thought things could happen this fast on the island.

Jason shook hands with the two boys and walked away with long, graceful strides.

"Do you want to do something else?" asked Johnny.

"Can we still go to the lighthouse?"

"Sure, but it's about a half a mile walking distance from here. We'll have to leave our bikes here, since we have to go along the beach."

Once they were past the bay, the boys could see the top of the lighthouse again. The closer they got, the more of the structure appeared in front of them. Finally, they saw the whole building. The squatty tower stood on a rocky point of land at the northeastern tip of Long Island. Ever since Columbus's arrival this place was called Cape Santa Maria. The lighthouse was painted with white and red horizontal stripes. It was erected on a huge concrete base that was about twenty-five feet high. Michael climbed the stairs that led up to the entrance gate. The boy wanted to go in, but the metal door was locked.

"I don't think you can go in," said Johnny.

"Bummer, I would have loved to climb up to the top."

"Did you see that brass plate above the door?"

Michael looked up and saw a plate that had turned completely green. Still, he could read the name of his father clearly, with his date of birth and death. The latter was also his birthday. A strange feeling came over Michael. So many times he'd wondered where his father might be. Now, he was standing by his grave, the end of his quest. Yet, something deep inside him stubbornly refused to think that he knew everything there was to know about his dad. His mother had admitted as much to him: there were still many unanswered questions. Michael wanted to find out all the answers. Standing at the foot of the lighthouse, he was reminded once again of the ghost story. It became more and more fascinating to Michael. Maybe there was some clue in the story that could tell him something else about his dad. And whatever that might be, Michael would do anything to discover it.

TWELVE

It was already late in the afternoon when Michael came home. From a distance he could hear Jane Rogers's voice. She was just saying goodbye. Michael saw her climb on her moped and ride away.

"Have a good day, Mom?"

"Can't complain. The house is all clean. The garden looks great. And we stocked the pantry and the fridge. Now we can relax. But I have a terrible headache. Listening to Jane talk all day was a bit much. How was your day with Johnny?"

"It was a really interesting day. I saw a ton of the island."

"Was Johnny fun to hang out with?"

"Well, he's an okay guy, but I don't think he'll be my best friend any time soon. He knows almost everything, but he's not very adventurous."

"I would have thought as much," Patricia said. "You set a pretty high standard for the people around you. Just like your dad. The apple doesn't fall far from the tree, I suppose," Patricia chuckled. Then she waved Michael into the house. "Come on. There will be swarms of mosquitoes in a little while."

"Mosquitoes? I don't see any."

"Just wait a minute, and you'll feel them. By nightfall those little beasts get very active."

Michael followed his mother through the screen door.

"Mmmmm, it smells so good in here," he hollered. "What's in the oven, Mom?"

"Lobster tails in garlic sauce."

"Wow, that's the first time you've ever made that."

"I didn't get them, Jane did."

"Isn't lobster really, really expensive?"

"Not on this island, Michael. They're really easy to catch out here. It gets pricey for people who want to buy them in America or Europe."

"And what kind of salad is that on the table?"

"That's coleslaw. It's a mixture of cabbage and a little mayonnaise. Cabbage grows very well here. You can buy it everywhere."

"Can I have something to drink? I'm really thirsty."

"There's a big pitcher of iced tea in the fridge."

"Iced tea? Don't we have any coke or lemonade?"

"No, sweetie, that's too expensive."

"How weird is that? What's expensive at home, is cheap out here, and the other way around."

"That's because of the cost of shipping things and all the middlemen who get the goods from one place to the other. Understand?"

The boy nodded.

"When will dinner be ready?"

"Not long. Just a few more minutes."

Michael walked over to the bookshelves. He wanted to read a bit, but the shelves were empty.

"Mom," he called out, "where are those books you told me about on the boat?"

"Your father's books? I was wondering about that today, too. When I left, I couldn't possibly take them, so I asked Morris, the house sitter, to take care of them, but apparently they disappeared."

"When will you see Morris to ask?"

"Jane told me he died two years ago. But don't worry, those books will show up. Did you meet Jason today?"

"Yes, I did, and tomorrow he's going to teach me how to dive."

"Tomorrow?"

"Yeah, I'm meeting him at the swimming pool by the marina at eight."

"Well, you sure aren't wasting any time," Patricia said. "You are starting to take more and more after your father with each passing day. Where will it end?" she asked, hoping that her smile would hide her concern.

Michael laughed. The implication of Patricia's last remark had gone over his head.

In the morning, Michael sat next to Jason at the edge of the swimming pool.

"Michael," Jason said, "I've been a scuba diving instructor now for ten years, but I've never had someone who made progress as rapidly as you did. You were able to perform all the basic exercises perfectly in less than an hour. And you haven't even been swimming in the past ten years. Obviously you retained everything. I think you're ready for your first open water dive with scuba gear."

"When can we do that?" Michael asked enthusiastically.

Jason looked at his watch and hesitated for a second.

"Around ten," he said, "a boat will leave with a couple of tourists who want to go diving. I think there are a few open seats. You can come. I just hope Mr. Dulles won't mind."

"Is he the other manager?"

"Not quite. He's more like Mr. Braunschwein's assistant. He's a Vietnam veteran. When he got back to the States, he didn't feel like he fit in anymore, so he drifted down here. Now, he just does whatever his boss tells him to do. He'll do anything Mr. Braunschwein asks. But with us, he's arrogant. It's really annoying. What can you do, though? He pays us, so we keep quiet. We don't want to lose our jobs. If you father had not been killed in that accident, then …"

"Jason," says Michael, suddenly remembering the lighthouse, "you must have heard about this ghost tower?"

"Of course, everybody on Long Island knows about the tower;

some people say there's a spooky light shining there at night."

"What do you think about that?"

"Well, for starters, Michael, I've never seen that light with my own two eyes. On the other hand, I do live on the other side of the island and I know a number of people who swear they've noticed a strange glow up in the tower at night, sailing in from the ocean. However, I also happen to know those people have often had one too many drinks when they tell those stories."

"So how often have they seen this light?"

"More than once."

"Do you think there could be a real ghost?" Michael asked.

Jason smiled. "Michael, honestly, I don't know. If there is one, I certainly won't be giving him any trouble. I'm never in that area at night. So why worry?"

Michael was on the verge of asking another question about his father, when a car drove up. It came to a halt right by the wharf and three men got out. Each carried a diving bag. These were the people Jason was waiting for.

"Welcome aboard," he called. "We should be able to leave right away. I'm not expecting anybody else."

Then Jason turned to Michael and said, "Release those ropes and climb aboard. Let's get out of here."

At that moment, a voice called out from the distance.

"Jason! Did that little one sign up?"

An overweight man stepped out of the marina bar. He wore long, dark pants and a beige camouflaged shirt. His hair was cut short. On his nose he had a pair of mirrored sunglasses, making it impossible to see his eyes.

"This boy is coming along for his first open water tests," Jason answered, clearly irritated. "He's a very good diver."

"I didn't ask if he's a good diver. I asked if he's registered. I want to know if he paid."

"No, but his father instructed me for free. I owe him this."

"I'm not interested in personal accounts. If the boy didn't pay, you'll have to pay for him, or else he's not going. Is that too hard for you to understand?"

Michael was furious. Jason didn't have to tell him that this guy was Dulles. Too bad Michael was just a kid. Otherwise he would have taken that bully down a notch or two.

It wasn't until Dulles disappeared that Michael dared to look at Jason again. The boat was slowly floating away from the dock.

"Some other time, Michael," Jason said. "I'm sorry, but I can't pay for your dive. That doesn't mean it's never going to happen, though. And as far as that baboon is concerned, sooner or later he'll get exactly what he deserves, I guarantee you."

Michael watched the boat for quite a while. All these images were swimming around in his head. So much had happened since he arrived on Long Island. And he'd learned so much, too. But it only brought up more questions. Michael was becoming quickly convinced that this gorgeous island had something to hide. There was the lighthouse that had never worked. Then there was the ghostly light at certain times. And all this was happening at the spot where his father lay buried. He wanted to know all the ins and outs of the matter, and soon. He didn't have a clue as to where it might lead, but he wanted to find out a whole lot more about his father's life. And, maybe even something about his death too …

Immediately, Michael wondered where to get started. To get to the lighthouse in the darkness seemed awfully difficult, plus it was too far to go at night, but that high hill with the little pavilion wasn't far from his house. Maybe from there, with a pair of binoculars, he could see something. He decided that he would keep an eye on the lighthouse from the top of the hill every night, starting tonight. He was hoping his mom wouldn't get too suspicious about his not being around, and, even more so, that it wouldn't be too long before he saw something that would give him an answer.

THIRTEEN

Tuesday night, August 11

For the fifth time, Michael climbed the hill to the pavilion. The sun had already disappeared behind the horizon. From the bench, Michael enjoyed the wonderful view of the northern part of the island.

To the west, yellow, orange and purple stripes colored the sky. These were the last colors of the day. He could still see a little stretch of the sandy beaches and the mangrove swamps by the Caribbean. But within a few minutes, it would be just as dark as it was on the east side. There, the Atlantic relentlessly pounded the rocks and the cliffs. The wind, too, came from that same direction. It provided a welcome cool-down and it chased away the mosquitoes and the sand fleas. Otherwise, Michael wouldn't have been able to stay for more than fifteen minutes.

In the distance, Michael could see Long Island's short north coast, and on its eastern tip, Cape Santa Maria. Through his binoculars, he could see the white top of the lighthouse. Bring it on, ghosts, he thought. If nothing had happened by the day after tomorrow, he would quit, he decided.

Michael was thinking about the diving lessons Jason had given him, and the two open water dives he had done today. He was happy that Dulles left for Nassau and would be gone for a couple of days. That way, he could finish his last two open water dives tomorrow and get his certificate. He never knew that scuba diving was so much fun. It was too bad that he still had not seen any dolphins, like his mom and dad had. Michael imaged that diving among those animals was fascinating. Michael closed his eyes and pictured himself swimming under water amid the dolphins. He exhaled deeply, and was happy.

Suddenly, he heard something humming in the distance. Michael thought it might be a small airplane several miles away passing over the island, as he had heard on previous nights. However, this time, it grew from a murmur into a low drone. Michael turned around, but didn't see anything. After a week on the island, Michael had heard so many of those little private planes flying over, that he'd practically stopped noticing them. But now it was evening and few planes passed by in the dark. Michael had heard that at night in the Bahamas, planes could only land in the big airports. None of the others had any lights, including the one on Long Island. But the sound of this plane kept on getting louder.

Michael turned around again and that's when he saw it. At the outermost tip of the island, there was a white glowing light. He picked up his binoculars and looked through them. A white mist surrounded the top part of the lighthouse, but it didn't look very spooky from above. Yet, Michael could easily image how someone at sea or on the beach could take it for a ghost. Especially if that person were superstitious. But from here the lighthouse looked more like a chimney where a strong light was beamed straight up from the inside. Yes, that was it! What he was seeing clearly had nothing to do with ghosts. But why would anyone want to shine this light at night?

Michael didn't have to wait long for his answer. To his left, the plane flew past him. He heard the roar of the motor, but he didn't see any lights. That was odd. Normally, every plane had to have its board lights on at night. The boy could hear the aircraft making a half circle in the distance. Then the sound faded. Not because the plane was flying off, but because it getting ready to land. Michael was getting more puzzled by the minute. How could the pilot safely land if the landing strip wasn't even lit? And why would he even attempt something like that?

Suddenly, a floodlight was switched on in front of the plane, but then the machine disappeared behind the trees. Then, Michael heard the aircraft landing.

Immediately, he looked toward the lighthouse, but it was dark; the light from before was gone.

Wednesday morning, August 12

Michael woke at the crack of dawn. He hardly took the time to eat his oatmeal. Then he biked north along the main road as fast as he could. Near the hotel, he left his bicycle behind, and continued on foot along the beach. When he finally arrived at the lighthouse, he looked at the structure from every angle. But from the ground, he couldn't see anything suspicious. Too bad it was impossible for him to see the top of the tower.

Michael began examining the immediate surroundings. There had to be an electrical wire somewhere to power the light he'd seen the night before. Somebody had switched it on and off, he was certain of that. But no matter how thoroughly he investigated the area around the concrete base, he couldn't find even the smallest trace of wiring.

His next thought was that it could be a remote control. He'd played with plenty of those kinds of toys. Maybe that's what was going on here. But where did such a powerful light get its energy? Unless … Michael thought back to Mr. Wagner's house, the house with those solar panels. That was it! On top of the lighthouse, but nicely hidden away, there had to be solar cells, batteries, a powerful lamp, and a small antenna. If he could fly over the lighthouse, not too high up, than he might be able to see the whole installation with his binoculars.

Instantly, Michael knew what to do. A few days before, Roby had invited him to take a tour around the island on his small airplane. This might be the perfect time to visit that kind man.

FOURTEEN

"It's so nice of you to take me along!" Michael shouted.

The boy had to raise his voice in order for Roby to hear him. The plane made a tremendous noise during take off.

Thirty minutes earlier, Michael arrived at Roby's. Roby was planting a banana tree. Immediately, he agreed to take Michael on a tour of the island in his Cessna. He didn't find anything odd in Michael's request to see the lighthouse from above. After all, it was also his father's grave.

It wasn't long before the old Cessna approached Cape Santa Maria. Michael noticed that the aircraft didn't even need to change direction.

"Roby, do you have a map of the island on board?"

"Certainly, son, over there in that folder. But first, take a look outside. We're about to circle the lighthouse."

They were at about three hundred feet when Roby began his circle. The elderly man flew clockwise so that the airplane's right wing pointed towards the base of the tower. That way Michael, sitting at the right side of the machine, could have a perfect view of the building below.

His suspicion was confirmed. The top of the lighthouse was in the shape of a tub. In it was some kind of installation. Michael looked through his binoculars. In the middle of the roof, he saw the white glass of a large flood light, and next to it, the dark surface of a solar panel. Opposite the panel, there was a metal case that probably held the batteries, and in the corner, a very small antenna.

"It's incredible how different the world can look from the sky, don't you think?" Roby asked.

"Absolutely," Michael answered. "You discover things you couldn't have seen any other way."

"That is so true!" Roby agreed.

But, Roby didn't have a clue as to what Michael really meant.

Then Roby changed direction. He flew south along the Atlantic Coast. He wanted to show Michael the dolphin bay and the Hotel Columbus. The boy was busy studying the map of the island.

"Wouldn't you rather look outside?" he laughed. "You can look at that map plenty later on."

Michael folded it up right away. Of course, Roby was right. Still, he was happy to have consulted the map just now. He had discovered something fascinating. Not only did he now know how the lighthouse light worked, he also knew what it was for. The lighthouse was located in a straight line with the landing strip. What was more, the landing strip was exactly between the two lighthouses. That certainly was too convenient to be a coincidence. Again, Michael thought of last night's airplane. How could the pilot have found the airfield if it hadn't been marked by a couple of lights? And those could only have come from the two lighthouses: the one at Cape Santa Maria in the northeast, which conveniently played the role of ghost tower, and the one in the southeast, that marked the entrance to the marina day and night. But, why had the pilot landed in such a mysterious manner? And why did he fly off after barely fifteen minutes? In a little while, Michael would ask Roby.

For the second time, the old man took a wide turn. They'd been following the Atlantic Coast of the island the whole time, but now Roby turned west and flew across the island. Michael saw the dark green brushwood with a blue hole here and there. Suddenly, the brush turned into a strip of sandy beach. Below the plane, the turquoise-blue water of the Caribbean spread out before Michael's eyes.

"Now we're flying north again," Roby said. "If you look ahead and squint a little, you can see a light gray stripe. That's the landing strip."

From this height, it was, indeed, easy for Michael to see, but he was paying close attention to the two lighthouses. There was no doubt about it. The two towers and the landing strip were clearly aligned.

"Michael, fasten your seatbelt," Roby said. "We're going to land."

"Already?"

"Yes, son, flying costs a lot of money. I told you just now you'd better look outside instead of studying that map."

Michael smiled.

A few minutes later, the machine touched down at high speed. Roby immediately pushed open the roof. When the plane was not in the air, the tiny cabin turned hot very quickly. Michael had already felt that right before take off.

The Cessna came to a halt. As soon as the motor was turned off, the boy was permitted to step down. Roby held out his hand to help him. This was the moment Michael had waited for.

"Roby," he said abruptly, "you know a lot about airplanes, right? Can I ask you something?"

"Whatever you want," the old man smiled, "I'll be happy to try to give you an answer."

"Tell me, Roby, why are there planes landing here at night?"

Michael was startled by Roby's reaction. His friendly face instantly vanished. Roby looked at the boy very earnestly. For a moment, it looked as if the elderly man didn't know how to respond.

"Michael," he said in a deep voice, "during the day this beautiful island is a little paradise for us. So enjoy it all you can. But at night, stay away from the airport, or your life won't be worth a dime!"

"But why?" Michael asked incredulously.

"Son, let me give you one more warning: don't stick your nose into things that don't happen in the light of day. I can't – and shouldn't – tell you any more than that."

With that, the conversation ended. Roby got into his mini-van and quickly said goodbye. After the vehicle disappeared around the curve in a cloud of dust, Michael got on his bike. During the short flight the boy had learned a lot. But again, many new questions had arisen. This island really did have something to hide. But right now, he didn't have the time to investigate. He had to get to the marina as quickly as possible. Jason would be waiting for him.

Later that afternoon the two scuba divers surfaced and dropped their mouthpieces. Finally, Jason spoke.

"Congratulations, Michael," he said, "you've earned your certificate. You performed all the tests brilliantly. I'll say it once again: you're my best student ever. A father's worthy son!"

Jason grabbed Michael's hand and shook it.

They began Michael's second dive, anchored at a depth of over thirty feet. First, Michael had to swim back and forth with the help of a compass. Then he had to take off his diving mask and put it back on. Finally, he had to stay motionless just above the ocean floor.

He performed each exercise with utmost ease. After that, Michael and Jason made a little underwater trip together. As required, they didn't go below sixty feet. During the trip, Michael saw a muraena for the first time. Although the long fish looked quite elegant, he thought it was a nasty monster. He was convinced the beast had mean eyes, and he didn't trust it. He would be scared to play with it, as Jason was doing. What's more, he didn't want to.

"Michael," Jason said, getting out of the water, "from now on, you can come along on every trip we organize. But if you want to dive deeper than sixty feet, you'll need to obtain a new certificate. And, between fifteen and fifty feet, you'll find the most beautiful coral reefs and the most colorful fish."

"As long as there are no muraenas," said Michael. "They really have a cruel looking mouth. I don't like them. They remind me of Braunschwein. No, I'll take dolphins any time. They look so likable, as if they're constantly smiling."

"Yes," Jason agreed, "it would be so much fun to dive among the dolphins again. It was really fantastic when your dad was around."

"Do you ever see any dolphins any more?"

"I do, actually. When we sail a bit further off the coast, they'll even swim alongside the boat for a while."

"Really?"

"Sure, but as soon as we reduce speed or if somebody jumps into the water, they're gone."

"When can we sail out far enough to meet the dolphins?" Michael asked suddenly.

"Usually, we only do that when we want to dive really deep. In order to get to a depth of a hundred feet, we have to go at least a mile off shore. During the trip there and back, we sometimes see dolphins. However, as a little reward for your splendid achievement today, I'll make a little detour. We might be lucky and see a couple of dolphins."

"Woo hoo!" Michael shouted.

"Raise the anchor. I'll start the motor."

Because it was a calm day, the Caribbean looked like a mirror. As the water got deeper, the ocean floor changed colors. First it was yellow, which slowly became light blue, then suddenly turned into dark blue.

"How come the water changes color here all of a sudden?" Michael asked.

"That's because the ocean rapidly gets much deeper out here. This is the edge of the plateau. Here it plunges straight down; that's why the color changes."

Just then, Michael heard a blowing sound coming from the side of the railing. Just below the surface, he saw a dark figure swimming forward quickly. A few seconds later, it surfaced. That's when Michael saw the likable snout and the typical dorsal fin.

"A dolphin," he shouted. "A dolphin at starboard!"

"Not so loud, Michael, you'll scare them away."

Jason, in the meantime noticed many more of them swimming toward the boat. Michael now spotted them as well. He counted at least seven. They took turns coming up to the surface to breathe. It looked as if they could keep up with the vessel effortlessly.

Suddenly, it happened again. In no time, the animals seemed to cast a spell on Michael. Just like at the aquarium, he became so captivated he could not contain himself any longer. The force was too strong. The boy grabbed his diving mask, put it on, and jumped from the moving boat. Instantly, he was among the dolphins. Jason, who had heard the splash, cursed. He immediately stopped the propellers.

The first things Michael saw, as soon as the bubbles around him were gone, were the dolphins' tails. Apparently, the animals had bolted because of his plunge.

Unexpectedly, one of the dolphins turned around and hesitated. Michael looked the dolphin straight in the eye and slowly started swimming towards it. Then, as though the animal recognized the boy, it started swimming in his direction. The next moment, they met. The dolphin let himself be touched and petted. It was as if they had known each other for years.

The other dolphins were now swimming back, one by one. Michael remembered diving into the aquarium, only this time he was surrounded by the blue water of the ocean and many more dolphins.

Finally, he grabbed the dorsal fin of that first dolphin, which started to slowly pull the boy along. First on the surface, then down below. A minute or so later, he resurfaced, right alongside the boat.

Jason watched the scene with wide eyes. Michael looked up at him, a bit fearful.

"Jason, are you mad?" he asked in a small voice.

"I should be very mad. You don't just jump from a moving boat. You could have gotten entangled in the propellers," he yelled from the boat with his hands on his hips. Then his face softened. "On the other hand, I'm completely astonished by what I've just seen. This is the first time the dolphins haven't disappeared when someone jumped into the water from a boat. And, I recognize the dolphin you were swimming with. Your father was there when he was born. He named him Derby. He was Gipsy's son, and, more importantly, he was your dolphin brother."

FIFTEEN

"Mom! Mom! You'll never guess what happened!"

Full of enthusiasm, Michael rode his bike into the yard yelling for his mother. He braked so abruptly that his rear wheel made a huge turn and almost flipped his bike over. He quickly jumped off his bike, which crashed down on the grass.

"Calm down, okay?" Patricia called. "Take it easy!"

"Mom, guess! What do you think happened?"

"You got your diving certificate!"

"Yeah! But that's only half the big news. There's something much more important."

"How would I know? Just tell me, please."

"I met Derby and he recognized me!"

"Derby! How do you know it was him?"

"Jason recognized him."

"Then I don't doubt it, though that's a little hard to believe. Think about it; it's been more than ten years since you last saw each other."

"Did Derby know me that well?"

"Certainly. He was swimming with you when you weren't even two weeks old. Derby was only four months old at the time. He was born in April. Your dad was there. Gipsy was his mother, remember? The dolphin who was there when you were born."

"Yes, Jason told me that too. But did you know Gipsy died? Two months ago, she was shot in Florida. It was in all the newspapers. Jason gave me this clipping. Here; look. But I have to give it back to him."

When Patricia read the article, she became very quiet. Michael saw tears in her eyes.

"Yes, Michael," she said, her voice shaky, "that is terrible. Gipsy was not only your father's favorite dolphin, she also was your dolphin mother. She was present during your birth and she taught you how to swim. That's why you're so good at diving."

"How?"

"Well, following the doctor's advice, when you were a few weeks old, I took you to this shallow, warm water in Mangrove Bay. You were floating and I supported your little back and tiny head with the palm of my hand. You flapped your arms and legs like crazy. Sometimes your head went under, but it didn't bother you at all. You were born under water, after all. You held your breath automatically. All of a sudden, Gipsy was there. Before I knew what was happening, she was swimming right past me. With her snout, she lifted you from my hand. At first, I was shocked and scared. But then I saw that she had simply taken over my job, and that she was much better at it. It was as if you understood each other. The next day, you were flapping your arms and legs so well that you could stay afloat for a little while without any support. Sometimes Gipsy lifted you up and let you tumble back into the water. Even though you kept on dipping, you were crowing with pleasure. The water was ninety degrees, so you could easily stay in for a long time. Eventually, you could float without any help. After that, she flipped you and taught you how to swim belly down. It didn't take long for you to learn that too. Next, you started clutching Derby's dorsal fin. Most of your physical strength was in those tiny little fingers of yours. And once you latched on to that baby dolphin, nobody could pry you loose. I took you to that same spot practically every day. You and Derby very quickly became the best of friends. You often dove down to the ocean floor with him, sometimes even six feet deep. I started wondering if you were a human being or a dolphin."

"How long did that last?"

"Almost three years. Ten years ago, the dolphins disappeared. The

Hotel Columbus opened its doors at Christmastime. The dolphins in the bay attracted a lot of tourists. But, just as your father had expected, all those people scared the animals off. We saw less and less of them. Then one day, in February, they were gone for good. Since then, nobody has ever seen them again. The hotel lost its main attraction, but its reputation was made. The tourists kept coming. And soon, the dolphins were completely forgotten. But, you started having problems. You were so used to the animals that you couldn't be without them. It seemed like your life force disappeared with the dolphins. You hardly ate anything and you were losing weight quickly. At one point, I was really scared you might not survive. The doctor who had helped us, moved away. And the new doctor didn't understand any of it. It got so bad that I had to take you to Miami. You were admitted to a hospital where they tube-fed you because you were so weak. Eventually though, you pulled through. But they advised me that you should never again have any contact with dolphins. They said it would be best to avoid water and swimming altogether. They were scared it would start all over again, and that perhaps nobody would be able to save you. That's why I tried to keep you away from the water. And why I never wanted to talk to you about dolphins. I was so afraid that I would lose you, just like I had lost your Father. Does that make sense?"

'Yes, Mom, absolutely. However, I'm really glad I jumped in the water with those dolphins back at the aquarium. Wasn't that proof that those doctors were wrong?"

"Agreed, Honey - though it did cost me a trip to the Bahamas."

"But, Mom, coming here got me diving again. And I met Derby. It was so fantastic. I was swimming and diving with him for more than thirty minutes. Incredible. When I got out of the water, he didn't want to let go of me. But I didn't have any choice - Jason had to get back by a certain time."

"Did Derby swim away?"

"No, he followed us until we were in the marina. That's where we said goodbye. I know for sure he'll be around. Jason saw him swim away in the direction of Mangrove Bay. Maybe I'll go visit him there tonight. But now I want to ride over to Roby; I want to tell him everything. He'll be so surprised!"

When Michael had left on his bike, Patricia once again picked up the clipping Michael had brought home. She looked at the date: Friday, June 26th. She took out her journal and looked for the date of Michael's terrible dream. Immediately, she saw that not only were the two dates the same, but they'd happened at the exact same time. Patricia stared at the horizon for a long time, lost in thought.

"Yes, Roby, and after dinner I'm going to bike over to Mangrove Bay. I'm pretty sure Derby will be there. He used to swim with me there when he was a baby dolphin with his mother. My mom told me about it."

Sitting at Roby's terrace with a glass of iced tea in front of him, Michael was explaining everything.

"But Michael," the old man interrupted, "it's nearly sunset and Mangrove Bay is very close to the airport. I hope you didn't forget my warning from this morning."

Michael let out a sigh.

"I can't even visit my dolphin brother?" he exclaimed. "What's going on at this airport anyway? Come on, can't you tell me?"

Now it was Roby's turn to sigh. The man realized he couldn't keep the boy in the dark. If he didn't tell him something, Michael would probably investigate on his own, which would be really dangerous. Reluctantly, Roby decided to level with Michael.

"Look," he said, finally, "if you promise to keep away from the airport after sunset from now on, I'll tell you a few things. Agreed?"

Michael nodded.

"Well, as I told you the other day, for years the Bahamas were one big pirate den. The buccaneers used the hundreds of little islands to hide out and store provisions. The pirates would strike all around the Caribbean, plundering ships and attacking coastal villages. They appeared and disappeared quickly, and they found shelter in the Bahamas. Just like today, most of the islands were sparsely populated. When the pirates showed-up, they didn't bother the local population, and the Bahamians pretended they hadn't seen anything. This state of lawlessness lasted a couple of centuries, until the British, French, and Spanish navies succeeded in purging the Caribbean of piracy."

Michael already knew what Roby was telling him, but what did pirates have to do with airplanes? Fortunately, Roby continued his tale.

"These days, we're more or less back in the same situation. Only this time, we're not dealing with pirates, but with drug smugglers. The smugglers usually use small airplanes to transport their goods to the U.S. from Columbia where they produce cocaine. But, it's a long distance between Colombia and fueling is a big problem. It's impossible for these small aircrafts to make it from South America to North America in one shot, so they need to refuel. Since the southern Bahamas are about halfway, that's where they make a stop. The pilots fly by night with their lights turned off in an attempt to be inconspicuous. When they get to the island where they will refuel, the ground lights come on so they can land more or less safely. Then, a car drives up to the plane with a barrel of fuel. It takes less than ten minutes to fill up the plane's tanks. The pilot pays his helpers, usually in dollars, but sometimes in cocaine. Then he takes off and keeps flying until he gets to the United States."

"What about the police?" Michael asked. "Don't they know about this?"

Roby burst out laughing.

"The police know everything about it, but they hardly ever interfere."

"So you're saying the police aren't doing anything?"

"They're scared to take action, and what's more, they are not allowed to step in."

"How can that be?" Michael exclaimed, outraged.

"Well, put yourself in the policeman's place for a minute. He may have a nice uniform, but he doesn't make a whole lot of money. He knows just as well as I do that the drugs smugglers regularly use the landing strip to refuel, but, just like all the others that know, he doesn't do anything, because he knows that if he took any action, he would either get shot right there, or get killed in an 'accident' a few days later."

"Killed in an accident?"

"Yes," said Roby, "the smugglers make sure the man gets killed, but they make it look like an accident."

"No!"

"Those guys will do anything. They're merciless because they have too much to lose. Do you know how much money they get for a plane load of drugs?"

"No, I don't."

"Sometimes it's millions of dollars. There is so much money at stake, they won't allow even the smallest mistake."

"But why can't the government do anything about it? If the police officer told his superiors in Nassau that these smugglers are landing here on a regular basis, wouldn't they take action?"

Again Roby laughed.

"No, son, that won't happen."

"But why not?"

"Because the policemen don't want to run the risk of getting relocated to a desolate island."

"How come?"

"Sometimes the smugglers give a nice sum of money to the chief of police in the capital. They expect him to keep his subordinates in check. Every police officer is very aware of this situation. That's why they're not taking any action."

By now Michael understood almost everything. Yet he wanted to know a few more details.

"So tell me, Roby, do you know who is helping to supply the smugglers with fuel here on Long Island?"

"Michael," the man said, "now listen carefully. I don't want to know. I don't want to have anything to do with them, and that goes both ways. I'm sure I know them, because everybody knows everybody else on this island. If we run into each other during the day, they'll certainly be friendly, but if they ever saw me at the airport at night while they're doing their thing, I know I won't live much longer. I'm giving you good advice, and I mean it: don't play with fire and stay away from the airport after sunset."

The boy nodded. He understood. But how much of this warning he would take to heart was a very different matter.

SIXTEEN

Tuesday, August 18

The sun turned into a red ball, hanging just over the bushes. The quiet of night descended upon the island.

Just as he had done a week ago, Michael was once again on the look out, but this time, he was much closer to the airport.

Over the past few days, he had explored the area around the landing strip. He wanted to find a good spot where he could spy on the smugglers without any risk of getting caught. That, however, had not been an easy task. Shrubs and small trees enclosed the airfield, but they were too far from the airstrip for him to get a good view. If he wanted to be closer, he'd have to expose himself. He thought that was too dangerous though. He considered climbing a tall tree – from there he would have a great view - but it would be very uncomfortable. It would be okay for a few moments, but not for a few hours. Finally, he had discovered a small hill at the edge of the runway. It was overgrown with low bushes. In reality, it was just a pile of dirt and rubble. When they were building the airport, they probably dumped the surplus materials and soil there and bunched it up with a bulldozer. Whatever the case, that morning Michael had climbed it and he immediately knew that he'd found his hiding place. Then he went home and came back in the late afternoon.

Michael carefully hid his bike in the bushes. Because he did not know how long he would be there, he'd packed a chunk of bread, three small bananas, and a can of soda. His faithful binoculars were around his neck.

Michael waited for over an hour, hoping a plane would make a stopover tonight. The last time it happened was Tuesday, and, by coincidence, he had learned from Jason the Tuesday before a plane had also stopped. Chances were good that it would happen today as well.

Over the last few days, Michael had mounting suspicions about who was involved based on his clues. The person who made sure the two lighthouses and the runway lined-up had to be involved with the smuggling one way or another. The person was probably also involved with burying his father in one of the lighthouses. And, the person probably created a ghost story to keep the local population at a safe distance. Michael suspected that Braunschwein was somewhere in the equation.

Michael realized that this time he was playing with fire. His mom would be furious if she ever found out what he was up to. But the worst part was breaking his promise to Roby. Yet, Michael couldn't help himself. Something had pushed him to this place - and it wasn't just his curiosity. No, a voice from deep within had urged him to make this dangerous adventure. Not only would he learn more about his father, but it might bring him closer to him. Michael didn't quite understand how this would be possible, especially since his dad was actually buried underneath the lighthouse, but he was certain about it.

Again, Michael looked in the distance. The sun had set completely. There was hardly a breeze. Michael slathered himself with bug repellant. The airport, after all, was on the Caribbean side of the island, which always had less of a breeze.

Mangrove Bay wasn't far from Michael's hiding place. Now that the last sunlight had disappeared in the west, he could no longer see the bay. During the past week, Michael had gone swimming practically every day, sometimes for hours on end. He spent all that time with Derby. Just as Michael expected, the dolphin turned up again in Mangrove Bay. The animal recognized him from a distance and swam towards Michael in a straight line. Michael had gone in the water with his snorkeling equipment. The dolphin simply would not let go of him. Even when Michael went diving in the ocean with Jason, Derby was there. As soon as the boat left the marina, the dolphin appeared. The animal followed them until they came to their diving spot. And once the boy was underwater, the dolphin swam beside him constantly. Those had been glorious dives, each and every one of them.

But something else was happening. Each time Michael was underwater with Derby, it seemed as if their relationship deepened, as if they understood one another more and more. It wasn't just that they could communicate with each other - no, that wasn't it. Something much deeper was happening. Over the past few days, an invisible bond had developed between them. Or, perhaps, it had always been there. It was almost as if the dolphin could read his mind. And, furthermore, Michael felt as though he could feel what went on inside Derby. It was as if they'd been together for many years, which wasn't really that surprising, considering he had been in contact with dolphins from the time he was in his mother's belly to the day that they had left the island. When he was born under water, they were close by. They had taught him how to swim and dive when he was a baby. And he had played and romped around with Derby for years. They even called this animal his 'dolphin brother.' No, it wasn't surprising that Derby and Michael developed such a strong bond. Now that they'd found one another again, it started all over. Michael was wondering what else might be possible when he heard cars approaching and his ears perked up.

Two cars drove across the bridge that connected Hog Island to the big island. They were approaching the airport. Fortunately, it was completely dark. Then, the clouds shifted and the whole area was bathing in the silvery light of a full moon. Perfect to see everything,

Michael thought, but at the same time dangerous. He might be seen. He would have to be careful.

When the cars drove up the runway, the boy saw that their lights were off. No doubt about it, he thought, these are the ones. One of the vehicles stopped at one end of the runway, its nose turned in. The second car drove down to the other end. It passed by Michael's little hill by less than fifty feet. At the end of the strip, the vehicle turned around and came to a halt. The two cars were now parked at both ends of the runway, facing each other. Michael didn't understand why they were doing that. He made a mental note to find out later.

It was quiet again. The only thing Michael could hear was the chirping of the crickets. Two men were talking by the car closest to Michael, but he was too far away to hear what they were saying. For a minute, Michael wanted to sneak up on them, but he quickly realized that that would be a foolish thing to do. He stayed still. He could witness enough from here. The only thing he regretted was that he couldn't see the lighthouse from here. He wondered if the lights were on yet. From here, they could be easily turned on by remote control.

Suddenly, Michael heard the familiar drone of an airplane engine. Almost simultaneously the cars' headlights flashed on. That way, both ends of the runway were illuminated. Finally, Michael understood. That was how the pilot could see the beginning and the end of the strip.

Meanwhile, the noise of the engine became louder and louder. The aircraft couldn't be far from the ground. Michael looked in the direction of the sound and saw the plane's floodlight come on. It lit a large part of the runway. Michael ducked his head. A moment later, the plane's tires hit the ground with a dull squeak.

By the time the machine passed by Michael's hideout, it had already lost much of its speed. It finally came to a stop, some three hundred feet further down the runway. The cars' headlights went dark again. The two men drove up to the plane. Now Michael could see it was a pick-up truck. A large drum stood in the back. The car parked next to the plane. The pilot climbed out and unscrewed something on top of the wings. The fuel tank cap, Michael thought. The driver of the car took a nozzle and stuck it into one of the wings. Then, he jumped up on the car and started moving a handle attached to the drum up and down. That had to be a hand-pump. In the meantime, the pilot was talking to the other man. Even using his binoculars, it was impossible for Michael to recognize the three figures. He could see that the man at the pump was rather large. The one talking to the pilot looked very fat. This almost confirmed his suspicions, but he wasn't a hundred percent certain quite yet.

All of a sudden, the man stopped pumping. The pilot interrupted his conversation and walked over to the other wing. A few moments later, they started filling up the plane's second fuel tank. Michael was surprised to see how fast it all happened. Apparently, they wanted the stopover to be as short as possible.

When the second tank was full, he saw the pilot hand a package to the fat man and shake his hand. The pilot immediately got into his plane and started the engine. The pick-up drove away and positioned itself once again at the start of the airstrip.

The plane slowly taxied to the left side of the runway. It came by Michael's hill a second time, but now drove much slower. At the end of the strip, the plane stopped for a few seconds. Then it made a 180-degree turn. The lights on the pick-up splashed on. The engine began roaring ferociously and the aircraft burst forward. It raced past Michael, the engine howling. A moment later, it lifted off and was gone.

The boy watched the car pass by, and soon the pick-up drove off, too. A few minutes later, the airport was quiet.

Now it's my turn, Michael thought. Crouching, he snuck down the little hill. At the bottom, he dashed into the shrubs. There, he found the path and picked up his bike. Five minutes later, Michael reached the road. He stopped for a moment to make sure nobody was around to see him. Then he mounted his bike. As fast as he could, and without any lights on, he peddled to the bridge. It wasn't until he crossed the bridge and reached the main road that Michael felt any relief. He looked at his watch and saw that it was really late. Quickly, he turned right and rode south to go home. However, he didn't notice the two men from the airport stepping out of the bushes some hundred yards behind him.

When the boy had driven some distance, the first man spoke to the second man.

"See, I was right. I thought that kid was hanging around the airport a bit too much the last couple of days."

"You were right, Charlie," said the other one. "That wasn't a bad idea, to wait around out here a little longer. I wonder where he was hiding all that time. Well, whatever, he knows too much. He's got to go!"

"Can I take him on, boss?"

"No way. You know I don't want any more murders around here. That would frighten the tourists, or lure the Special Squad from Nassau over here. Just leave it to me. I know just the person to fix this little chore."

"Scarecrow?"

"You guessed it! It's high time we have another stab at getting him out of the slammer. I'm sure the Big Boss can do it this time. John Scarecrow is just the guy to arrange a couple of inconvenient little accidents. When the plane comes in next week with the big cargo, we'll make sure there aren't any more peeping toms hanging around. Come on, let's go. Remind me to send a message to Colombia tonight, okay?"

SEVENTEEN

Friday, August 21

Michael was resting in the shade of a large sea grape bush. The sun was high in the sky and it was swelteringly hot. Some ninety feet away, Derby was cackling in the water.

"Come on, Michael," he seemed to be saying. "Come out and play with me. Are you tired already?"

Michael was exhausted. He'd been in the water with Derby for hours. The muscles in both of his arms were sore. He felt worn out and needed to rest. Eventually, the dolphin gave in and left him alone. Again, the boy was thinking about this special day. Today was his birthday, but it no longer felt like a day to celebrate. Thirteen years ago, he was born in this place, but his father had died that same day. Michael hadn't known this before, and now he knew why his mother often had had tears in her eyes on his birthday. It had always puzzled him. Once, he had even got mad at her about it. Now he understood.

Michael could see Mangrove Bay stretching out before him. From here, he had a great view of the spot where he was born. He saw Derby still swimming in circles in the middle of the bay. Michael was thinking of his father. The man died the moment his son came into the world, and not very far from here.

Slowly, Michael let his eyelids droop, until there were only two slits left, just enough to keep track of Derby a little while longer. But when his eyes were completely closed, Derby came very close and called him. Almost against his will, Michael obeyed. Derby dragged Michael through the water at a dizzying speed. It turned from turquoise into indigo, then purple, then black. Then the dolphin pulled loose. Miel was all alone in the dark, warm water. In the distance he heard a pounding that became louder and louder. Somewhere a heart was beating calmly and regularly. Then, a light flashed in his eyes. The boy looked up and saw a blue opening. Two divers were staring at him. Then he saw something terrible. The second diver was fiddling with the diving gear of the first one. Michael wanted to call out, but no sound came out of his mouth. The first diver started shaking violently and tried to swim upwards. His mask fell off. Michael suddenly recognized himself, only many years older. Then he realized the man was his father. Michael wanted to come to his rescue, but he couldn't. He was stuck. His heart started to beat very fast. He was slowly sliding down. His legs were being pulled down, down, down. The boy looked up again and saw that the two divers were swimming up, but they were locked in a struggle. He yelled: "Dad, Dad, Dad!!!" But the blue opening was gradually closing up, and Michael was losing his strength. He felt like he was being squashed from all sides. Then, suddenly, he heard a friendly voice.

"Turn, Michael, turn around. Come on, hurry up or you won't make it." He turned around. It was difficult to move, but he did it. Then whatever was pulling him before was back. Suddenly, his surroundings turned light blue. In front of him was a gray silhouette. The voice that had just called to him, spoke a friendly greeting. He snapped loose and was lifted up. Then Michael saw that he was not alone. Next to him, someone else was ascending. His father was there, but did not see him. They were rising, but not fast enough yet. Unexpectedly, with a deafening sound, they broke through a glass wall together. His lungs filled with air. And then, as loudly as he could, Michael screamed, "Daaaaaaaaaad!" The man lifted his head and smiled at him. Michael wanted to grab him, but abruptly he disappeared. Instead, he saw the gray silhouette, which slowly changed into a dolphin. Michael noticed the scar underneath the eye. Then he heard a bang, and another, and another. Everything turned blood red. At the top of his lungs he yelled: "Mou-Mou!!!"

At that moment, Michael woke up. The boy was completely exposed to the sun and was lying in a pool of his own sweat. The sun had shifted to a different position and the shade of the bush had changed with it. Ninety feet away, Derby was splashing up a storm. He was chattering a mile a minute. "Did you understand? Did you get it?" he seemed to be asking.

Had Michael been dreaming or had Derby been telling him something in his sleep? If the latter was true, then his father was not killed in an accident when Michael was born, but murdered. And that meant something very strange had happened right before his birth. Still slightly dizzy, Michael stood up and went to his bike. He would not rest until he knew every little detail about this business.

It took a long time until the tiny dot turned into a boat. Too long, as far as Michael was concerned. But then the ship started getting bigger quickly. Finally, it moored at the dock, right under his nose.

"Can you grab the ropes?" Jason called out to him.

The ropes flew toward Michael. While he tied them to the dock, the first divers jumped from the boat. Jason turned off the engine, and was the last person to come ashore.

"Happy birthday, man! How are you doing today?"

"Okay," Michael held back.

"Just okay? You only have one birthday a year, you know! So you've got to make the best of it," Jason said firmly.

"Look, Jason, that's exactly my problem," Michael said. "It's just that too much has happened on the day I was born. It'll never feel right again."

"I know what you mean," Jason said, suddenly softer. "I think about it every year too. You know I knew your dad pretty well. Thanks to him, I now have this job as a diving instrctor. He taught me how to dive because when your mom was pregnant, your dad didn't want her to go scuba diving any longer. That's how I became his assistant."

"I know, Jason. That's exactly the reason I came to see you. You were with my father practically every day. Can you tell me if he had any enemies here?"

"Enemies?" Jason exclaimed. "Why would you ask that, Michael?"

For a moment, Michael was at a loss for words. He wanted to tell Jason what he had experienced when he was asleep, but maybe Jason wouldn't believe him. Maybe Jason would laugh.

"Well, you know," the words came hesitatingly.

Jason looked at him, shaking his head.

"Listen, Michael," he said, "your father was a great guy. In the twelve months he lived here on the island, he did a lot for us. He didn't just love dolphins, he loved people. That's why he had so many friends. Sure, some guys were mad at him a couple of times. But enemies? I don't think so. As a scientist he loved this island, and the locals too. He felt at home when he was with us. He never avoided our parties. He was different from the others who came, and they looked down on him. Those folks were here either to have fun or to make money. They would never seek us out. But, your father did. And those who lived in the development thought he was weird. Some even considered him a traitor. After all, he was the one who encouraged us to stop buying everything in their stores. Instead, he said we should organize. We should buy the goods in bulk ourselves, just like most of the others did. Well, that didn't go over so well with the rich shopkeepers. They were able to make a lot of profit because we were divided."

"Why's that?"

"Well, the store owners ordered their goods in Nassau and sold them here for almost double the purchase price."

"So why didn't you guys order them yourselves?"

"We couldn't. You had to buy a large number of things in one go, and also pay up front. That was only possible if we did it together and nobody had ever explained to us how to do that. Your father helped us a great deal."

"So that means the store owners didn't like my dad very much."

"You can say that again, Michael. But it was especially the development managers who were really mad at him a few times."

"What did he do to them?" Michael asked.

"For starters, he had their water collection project put to a stop. Those guys wanted to get all the fresh water out of the ground. They wanted to sell it to the future residents of the development for high prices. But it would have made the water for the farmland too salty and all crops would have withered. As a scientist your father realized this in time. After that, he took the necessary steps with the Nassau authorities. You can easily guess the results."

"I sure can!" Michael exclaimed.

"And then there were the plans to build the hotel in a different location."

"Mom told me about that. Braunschwein wanted to put up the hotel by the dolphin bay."

"That's right, and your father fought this with all his might. He threatened to show his dolphin film in Nassau's highest circles. He knew they would take action. He wanted the whole area around the bay to be declared a nature reserve."

"How did the development managers react?" Michael asked.

"They got scared. The next day, they promised to give up their plans. But when your father died, there was no one to stop them. A few years later, they started building the hotel. And you know how that turned out. With the arrival of the tourists, the dolphins disappeared for good. Such a pity. So, your dad was right again."

"Jason," Michael asked after some hesitation, "can I ask you something really weird?"

"Yes, son, of course."

"Jason, could it be possible that they murdered my father because he had the guts to resist their plans?"

"Michael," Jason exclaimed indignantly. "This is not Nassau, you hear me. People don't murder other people here. And certainly not over a bunch of dolphins!"

"I have one last question, Jason."

"Yes, Mister Detective."

"Is there any chance my father ever had any trouble with drug smugglers?"

"What makes you say that?" Jason asked, almost angry.

"Well, Roby told me those people land here on a regular basis. And I thought that maybe my father ..."

"Well, you're wrong," Jason interrupted him. "Because there wasn't any drug smuggling in those days."

"No? Why not?"

"Because they were still busy building the airport. Now, stop talking all this nonsense. Your father was just the victim of a diving accident, and that was bad enough!"

Jason got up, clearly annoyed, and walked over to his workshop to fill up the air tanks. Michael stayed behind in despair, wondering if he was still on the right track.

EIGHTEEN

"Michael, you're so quiet," Patricia said to her son. "Can't you put on a happy face? We've been invited to dinner at Roby's, but you look like a thunder cloud."

"I'm sorry Mom, but I can't stop thinking about Dad."

"I understand. That's why I have always had such a hard time on your birthday, you know?"

"That's not just it, Mom. Can I ask you something else about when I was born?"

"Michael, I told you everything when we were on the plane. If you really want to know more, you can ask me anything later tonight, when we get home. But now we really don't have time. We have to get to Roby's; we're already late as it is."

But the boy insisted.

"Just one question, Mom. Maybe I didn't hear everything on the plane. Can you remember whether or not I turned right before I was born?"

Michael saw his mom suddenly blush.

"How did you know that?" she called out.

"Please just tell me if I'm right."

"Yes, you certainly did. Your birth almost didn't have a happy ending. But because you turned just in time, it worked out fine. But how did you find that out?"

"From Derby," Michael shouted with joy. "And that means that the rest of his story must also be true. Okay, Mom, that's all I needed to know. Let's leave for Roby's, or we'll be late."

Patricia shook her head. Now that Michael was spending all of his days among the dolphins, she wondered what other surprises her son would have in store for her. She hoped he would stay on the right track.

"Happy birthday," Donna, Roby's wife, said as she opened the door for Michael and his mother. "Come on in, we're so happy you could come for dinner at our house tonight."

The house consisted of one large space, with a brown, pitched roof. A table stood in the middle of the room and was already set for four people. To the right of the living room, was an open kitchen. From the doorway, Michael spotted a beautiful cake with thirteen candles. The other side of the room was an office. Roby was there, listening to the radio. Donna had to call him twice before he took off his headphones.

"Roby, our guests are here. Come on, turn off that radio."

Roby got up and apologized. He put the headphones on the chest of drawers and walked toward Michael and his mother.

"I'm sorry," he said. "I just heard some bad news on the radio."

"You'd better congratulate the boy on his birthday, instead of talking about the news!" Donna exclaimed snappishly.

"Oh, yeah, Michael," said Roby. "Happy birthday."

Michael saw Roby was distracted. Clearly, his mind was elsewhere. Michael wasted no time in asking what Roby had heard on the radio.

"Well, Michael," he said solemnly. "The first hurricane of the season is shaping up."

"So we'll have a big storm," Patricia said.

"We'll have some terrible winds and lots of rain, within a few days. That much is certain," Roby said.

"Yippee, we'll be seeing a hurricane," Michael cheered.

"Don't be so happy," Roby interrupted. "First of all, there's only a small chance of the hurricane coming close to the island. As long as it stays away more than three hundred miles, we'll only get a normal storm."

"And if it does come closer?" Michael asked, his eyes shining.

"Then, we'll have a really big storm. And if it moves across the island, there will be tremendous damage."

"Does that happen often?"

"No, luckily it doesn't. Maybe once every fifty years, at the most. It's a good thing the Caribbean is such a big place."

"Where is this hurricane right now?" Michael asked.

"At this moment, it's still very far away. A couple days ago, it started over the Atlantic, east of the Lesser Antilles. Today, those islands saw a lot of wind and rain. Fortunately, they won't suffer a whole lot of damage. The eye of the hurricane is far enough away from them. Meanwhile, it's moving slowly to the north, so it's not threatening us, yet. But if it curves further west, it might come pretty close."

"Ouch!"

'Well, don't worry. There's no reason to panic now. A hurricane can suddenly change course. And the radio keeps us posted all day long about a possible route of Delphine."

"Delphine?"

"Yes, Michael. It's customary to name the hurricanes. They often use the name of a girl. But be careful when she gets too close, 'cause she might be a real she-devil."

"And if these gentlemen don't come to the table right now, they will personally experience the wrath of a true she-devil!" Donna laughed.

NINETEEN

Saturday, August 22

Long trails of fog rose from the forested sides of the cone shaped volcano on the island of Gorgona. It was six o'clock in the morning. The first rays of sunshine illuminated the prison camp.

For decades, this small, far away island had been home to the most heavily guarded prison in South America. It was completely isolated at a distance of over thirty miles from the coast. It was nearly impossible to escape from there. Enormous schools of hungry hammerhead sharks mercilessly foiled every attempt of anybody who tried to get away by swimming. And because of the strong ocean currents, it was very difficult to reach the mainland by raft. And, the rare person who, against all odds, succeeded anyway, would find himself in a vast swampy territory full of giant snakes and alligators.

The island had a big volcano, surrounded by a dense tropical rainforest, crawling with poisonous snakes, crocodiles, and bats. Close to the narrow strip of sandy beach where the weekly supplies ship would moor, the prison camp stretched into a series of long barracks with three barbed wire fences pulsing with high voltage. Next to the camp, was a guard station. These stone buildings provided more conveniences than the wooden prison cells. The barracks smelled from the dampness. It rained practically every day on Gorgona.

At any given time, there were more than three hundred prisoners being held in the camp. They were all sentenced to a minimum of ten years. But this tiny devil's island was not just punishment for criminals. Soldiers and prison guards who'd been trouble on the mainland, were 'stashed away' on Gorgona for a couple of years. Then there was the prison commander. For him, this was not punishment; it was a necessary step in his climb up the military career ladder.

These were the last few months for Commander Garcia who'd been in charge at Gorgona for almost two years. He was expecting his promotion to the mainland any day now. Early this morning, the captain of the Libertad, the weekly supplies ship, had handed him a departmental letter. For an instant, he thought his time had come. But the notice was meant for some other lucky dog. The American John Scarecrow, who'd been locked up here for more than twelve years, He had unexpectedly received a commute of his sentence and could leave immediately. He was to leave with the Libertad tonight and would be a free man when he was dropped off at the docks at Buenaventura tomorrow night. This guy would end up back in the drugs business in less than a week; Garcia would bet a month of his salary on that. Experience had certainly shown that this Colombian island didn't improve its involuntary inhabitants very much. No, they picked up lots of new scams from their fellow inmates. The prisoners made so many new contacts, they could get back in the game in no time. But what could Garcia do about it? He was just an ordinary soldier who followed orders. So, he called a guard and assigned him the task of notifying Scarecrow, and asked him to arrange for the man's immediate departure.

Sunday, August 23

The sun had reached its highest point and sunk into the horizon while John Scarecrow stood at the ship's bow. His brown beard was covered with a thin layer of salt, deposited on his hairy face by the splashing ocean water. Dark sunglasses protected his eyes. It was the first time in many years he'd had the opportunity to stand in the light for such a long time. His lean body showed that he'd been forced to live on a restricted diet for a very long time. On Gorgona, all you got to eat was a bowl of rice and beans. Sometimes there was a smidgen of leathery shark meat.

He still didn't understand why he was released. Several times, Scarecrow had asked for a reduction of his sentence. He never received an official response. And yet, all the guards agreed that he was one of the easiest inmates. They never had any trouble with him. But that didn't seem to have the slightest impact. And now, suddenly, the prison door closed behind him. After all these years of bad luck, would he finally have a lucky break?

It started almost thirteen years ago to the day. He'd had left on his small yacht at full speed, from Long Island to Nassau. About halfway there, he crossed paths with a big sailing yacht. One of the Colombian sailors recognized his yacht. The big boat turned around and slowly but surely caught up with him. When it was alongside of him, there was the rattling of machine gun fire. A number of bullets hit the hull of his boat just below the water line. He knew it would sink within fifteen minutes. Resistance would be of no use whatsoever, so Scarecrow surrendered. On board the ship was El Carnicero, the infamous Colombian drug smuggler. He'd just delivered a cargo of cocaine to the United States and was on his way home. El Carnicero's big boss had been looking for Scarecrow for quite some time because he had a couple of accounts to settle with him. El Carnicero would personally deliver the American professional hit man to his boss.

But luckily for Scarecrow, it never came to that. Upon approaching the Colombian territorial waters, the sailing yacht ran into an ambush. Two Colombian police boats, informed by the American navy, were on the lookout. None of the passengers or crew members could escape. During a short but intense gunfight, El Carnicero was fatally wounded. All others were arrested, including John Scarecrow.

The police had found enough traces of drugs on the ship for everyone to be indicted. A few months later, the court sentenced John Scarecrow to fifteen years of hard labor. No matter how often he insisted he had nothing to do with the gang that was arrested, no one listened. He didn't exactly have a good reputation and was also found on board the smuggler's ship. So, he shared the fate of the others. He served his term on Gorgona.

By now the Libertad was beginning its last maneuver. The deckhands tossed the ropes on shore where another man tied them. The ship lined up alongside the dock, and the gangplank was pulled out. John Scarecrow, suitcase in hand, could step ashore a free man. For the first time in more than thirteen years, he felt at peace. But that didn't last long.

"Señor Scarecrow?"

A man dressed impeccably in a suit approached him. John Scarecrow only nodded in return.

"Congratulations on your release," the Colombian said. "The boss needs you for a new assignment. I'm sure you'll love every minute of it. Of course, there's no way you can refuse anyway. The boss didn't go through the trouble of getting your sentence reduced for nothing. Got it?"

John Scarecrow immediately understood. He had no other choice but to once more cooperate.

The man nodded and explained Scarecrow's assignment down to the last detail.

"Well, here you go, this is everything," the Colombian said finally. "A wallet with pesos and dollars, plane tickets, and a fake passport. I hope the photo is still okay; you've changed a bit in thirteen years. And don't forget: you're expected urgently. Here's our car. While I drive you to the airport, you can change into your new clothes. They're in the backseat. Okay?"

Half a minute later, the American limousine left Buenaventura's harbor at full speed.

TWENTY

Michael noticed the wind was blowing much harder than usual. If Roby hadn't mentioned it yesterday, he probably wouldn't have given it any attention. But the hurricane certainly was on its way. Even if not for the wind, Michael could tell something was up by what the people were doing. Everywhere he went, people were busy. Anything that could be blown away by heavy gusts of wind was taken inside, stowed away or tied down with strong ropes. The locals nailed large wood boards over the windows. The residents of the development, however, had aluminum panels at their disposal. They were fit into specially installed grooves in the doors and windows and secured. Roby, too, was busy with preparations. Michael asked him why the window had to be protected as well. Surly glass could withstand a bit of gusty wind?

"I don't think you realize how much power a hurricane can develop. At any moment, the wind can blow so furiously that it can pick up a human being easily and smash him to the ground dozens of feet away," Roby said. "The same thing happens to everything that's not nailed to the ground. We'll try to secure everything we own as best we can. But the bushes, branches, and even the trees might be ripped out of the ground and dragged along by the wind. When a heavy branch hits a window at the speed of one hundred miles an hour, I guarantee you the glass will shatter to pieces."

"Oh, now I get it," Michael said.

"But a broken window itself isn't the worst part, by far. Do you know what happens to the house when the windows break?"

"No."

"Well, the wind starts blowing in through the hole. Then you can be sure the roof and everything under it will go up in the air."

"How is that possible?" Michael asked. "I have a hard time imagining that."

"You don't need a whole lot of imagination to understand this. For instance, if you put a piece of paper on the ground and blow on it, it will hardly move. Bit if you lift it a tiny bit and blow underneath, it will fly very far away. Just try it."

Michael nodded, but apparently, Roby was not finished talking.

"Years ago, with my helicopter, I had to bring supplies to a village that had been ravaged by a hurricane a few days earlier. Most of the houses were hardly damaged, but the church's roof had blown off completely. Do you know how that happened?

Michael shook his head.

"You see, when the hurricane was on its way, all the residents gathered in the church. At the height of the storm, someone suddenly knocked on the door. He was late. At first, they didn't let him in. The people who were there were afraid that the wind would come in with him. When the late arrival kept insisting, some of the people started to feel sorry for him. Before the minister could stop it, someone unlocked the door. And that's when it happencd. The door flew open with a big bang. The beams in the roof started creaking. Everybody looked up and saw invisible hands lifting the roof. The next moment, it was gone. I saw with my own two eyes the twisted truss lying more than three hundred feet from the church!"

Michael whistled through his teeth and shuddered at the same time. Roby's stories were not for the faint of heart.

"But the most treacherous thing about a hurricane is its eye. That's the center of the storm. Strange as it may sound, in that part of the hurricane there is no wind and the sky is clear."

"Why is that bad?"

"Well, it's very odd. I've never seen it myself, but it happened to that town I just told you about. Apparently, the storm ended very unexpectedly. For nearly an hour, the weather was calm and beautiful. People thought it was all over and left the church. Everybody wanted to see what was left of their properties. But all of a sudden, the wind picked up. In only a few minutes, the storm was back at full speed. That was the second part of the hurricane. It raged just as badly and lasted just as long as the first part of the storm. Many of the people who had left the church were never found."

Again, Michael was shocked.

"So, Roby, what should you do during a storm like that? Is everybody going to get together some place or does everyone stay in their own homes?"

"That depends on how the hurricane develops," Roby answered. "Will it decrease or increase? Is it coming straight at us or will it pass at a distance? I think we'll know a lot more in the next couple of hours. In any case, if it gets too bad, they'll call everyone to come to the Great Cave. A few years back, when hurricane Hugo came straight at us in full force, we all got together in the Great Cave. We were lucky it wasn't really necessary that time. After a short night, we learned that Hugo had suddenly veered off its projected course. It had swept past the Bahamas in a wide curve. But if Delphine keeps coming in our direction, it's imperative that everyone gets to the Great Cave tonight. For us, that's the safest location during a hurricane. Maybe we'll see each other there tonight. Although I hope we don't. Now I have to get back to work. I've got to take down my radio antenna."

Michael got back on his bike. Everywhere people were working. The houses that normally looked so elegant, had lost their splendor. Everything movable had been locked away. Houses looked more like bomb shelters than residences. It looked like people were preparing for war.

A little later, Michael arrived at the marina. There it was more of the same: everyone was very active. They were trying to get as many boats ashore as possible. Obviously, the wind would be so strong that even the ships in this tiny little harbor would not be safe. Michael watched Johnny and his dad tie down their Boston Whaler, a big, shallow polyester boat. Jason, too, with a few helpers, was trying to secure his diving boat. Braunschwein and Dulles were keeping watch, as they always did, at the marine bar entrance. Dulles was the first one to spot Michael walking around. He turned to his boss.

"This Scarecrow guy, is he going to be here today?

"I don't know," said Braunschwein. "The regular Bahamas Air flight should have been here by now. Maybe they cancelled the flight at the last minute because of the hurricane. I think we should take matters into our own hands, just to be sure."

Then he called out to Michael, who immediately turned around. But when he saw who had called him, he approached the man very reluctantly.

"Hey kid," called Braunschwein. "I just heard the latest about the hurricane. It looks like the storm will be very close to the island by tonight. It would be good for you and your mom to get to the Great Cave early on in the evening since you live so far from there and you guys don't even have a car. This storm is very risky for a woman who's all by herself. You people should spend the night in the cave, you understand? Make sure to tell your mom!"

Michael nodded, but he wouldn't dream of taking this guy's advice. It was Tuesday again. He was sure there would be another drug runner's plane stopping by tonight. If Michael was stuck in the Great Cave so early, it would be impossible for him to sneak away. Could that be what they wanted? Either way, he certainly wouldn't tell his mother about it. Then he got on his bike and left.

With a smirk on his face, Braunschwein saw the boy disappear around the corner. Then Dulles spoke to his boss.

"Hey, Chief. Since when are you running a home for widows and orphans?"

"Hold it there, Charlie," said the fat man. "Hold your horses. Don't you get it? When that snot nosed brat is stuck in the Great Cave tonight, we'll have our hands free. I hope you didn't forget that we have something else coming by tonight, other than this hurricane?"

"Boss, you're a genius! Do you really think our plane will get here in this weather?"

"I was hoping it wouldn't, but the last I heard it left anyway. And we have to be prepared regardless of the weather."

"Yeah, sure, but what if the plane can't continue its flight? You know they're coming in with an extra-big load tonight."

"I know. That's why it would be better if we didn't have to worry about that rotten kid. Too bad they couldn't let Scarecrow go one day earlier. Then that troublemaker and his mother would already be out of the way."

TWENTY ONE

Michael was panting, riding up the hill. It wasn't so easy with the wind blowing in his face. He should have been back much earlier, but he wanted to see that enormous palm tree being chopped down. It was quite the spectacle. It was too bad about the tree, but Mr. Warren didn't have a choice. The tree hovered over his house. If the storm uprooted it, it would definitely fall onto his home. This hurricane was no laughing matter. Still, Michael had trouble imagining a storm being able to develop such power. So much that even sturdy trees could go flying just like that. The more Michael saw all the preparations, the more seriously he considered the hurricane.

"What kept you so long, Michael?" Patricia asked when he came home. "I talked to Mr. Braunschwein on the radio forty-five minutes ago and he said you were on your way. He also suggested we go to the Great Cave this evening. I think that's a good idea. But, we'll have to hurry. It'll be dark in a few hours and the hurricane is getting closer."

Michael swore under his breath. Braunschwein must have suspected that he wouldn't say anything to his mother. The boy quickly got off his bike. He wanted to park it in the bushes to be able to get away later on, but he was too late.

"Why don't you bring your bike inside," Patricia suggested. "Otherwise the hurricane will turn it into a heap of twisted metal."

"Maybe I can use it later on."

"No way, Michael. The wind will only get stronger. I don't want you to get flung to the ground, or worse. With this kind of weather, we could do without any broken arms or legs. Please do as I tell you, and get all the stuff I wrote down on this list."

Sulking, Michael took the list from his mother. Now he knew what he had to pack. The big beach bags, two air mattresses, two sleeping bags, all the flashlights and batteries he could find, the portable radio, canned and dry foods for a couple of days, extra clothing, and their waterproof jackets.

"Mom, do we really have to drag this stuff all the way to the Great Cave? Can't I put it in two backpacks? That's much easier to carry."

"That won't be necessary, sweetie," Patricia called. "Mr. Braunschwein promised to send someone. They'll pick us up in a car. We have to be ready at six."

Now Michael was really starting to get angry. It was going to be impossible to get out of this. He looked at his watch. There was hardly any time left to think of a good escape plan.

"Michael, come on, hurry up," Patricia called out. "This is not the time to be daydreaming!"

Reluctantly, Michael got to work.

Finally, the first raindrops fell from a sky that had turned black. The wind, too, was becoming more ferocious. Every gust bent the palm trees around the house. The rustling of the leaves being swept back and forth, grew louder. The ocean had turned almost as dark as the sky. White crested waves appeared everywhere in the water.

Thunderously, the waves crashed into the rocky coast, opening into a swirling mass that by now almost reached the edge of the lowest cliffs. A strong gust of wind carried a cloud of foam and ocean water inland. Meanwhile, the rain began pelting the roof. The rain washed all the salty deposits off the leaves of the plants.

A car slowly came to a stop in front of the house. Dulles was at the wheel. He saw three packages ready for pick up and he quickly loaded them in the trunk. He hurried because he hadn't taken a raincoat with him.

Patricia was working on her last chore. She nailed the front door shut with two heavy planks.

"Miss O'Neil, I hope you didn't forget to shut off the gas, the electricity, and the water?"

"No, Mr. Dulles, but thanks for reminding me. I went down the list of precautions twice. I don't think I forgot a single thing."

"Great. So, you guys should get in the car quickly."

Dulles hesitated. Then, in a very different tone of voice, he asked: "But where's your son? Isn't he coming?"

"Oh no, Mr. Dulles, we don't have to wait for him. Michael left about a half hour ago, on foot. He wanted to stop by his friend Johnny's on the way."

Dulles made a great effort to hide his anger. If that pesky brat really had left for the Great Cave on foot, all would be okay. But if the boy had other plans, Dulles would have a big problem.

Dulles jumped in the car. He turned on the ignition, put the gear in first and accelerated to full speed. Only then did Patricia realize something was not right. But she didn't have a clue what it could be.

TWENTY-TWO

Michael had been walking for quite a while. Without his bike and under the weather conditions, the mile long trip to the airport was not an easy one, but there was no time to lose. He wanted to get to the path he took last time before six o'clock, but he hadn't made it in time. Now, they would know what he was up to. And they would look for him everywhere. Especially when they discovered he never stopped at Johnny's.

Michael had been walking now for over thirty minutes. Finally, he crossed the little bridge connecting the main island to Hog's Island. Because of the bad weather, it was almost completely dark. He was getting drenched underneath his yellow rain slicker. Not from the rain, but from his own sweat. It was a good thing he'd thought to put on his diving suit at the last moment. Later on, when he was sitting down, he would still be nice and warm.

Just as Michael expected, his diving shoes were filling up with water. With each step he could hear their suction. His binoculars swung around his neck, his diving compass was on his wrist, and his diving knife was strapped to his right leg. In the pouch pocket of his slicker, Michael carried a small diving light and a few things to eat. He was glad he'd snagged these energy bars at the last moment from his mom's bag. Since they were sealed, he didn't have to worry about them getting wet.

He was just starting to wonder if the plane would even come in this stormy weather, when he spotted the path by the side of the road. A moment later, he disappeared into the bush. And just in time. Not twenty seconds later, over the roaring of the storm, Michael heard the sound of a car approaching. Instinctively, he lay flat on his belly.

Soon, two headlights pierced through the sheets of rain less than thirty feet away from him. Then the truck drove past. That was a lucky break; if the truck had been half-a-minute earlier, they would have plucked him right off of the road. But, he was safe - for now.

Because they were looking for him, Michael no longer doubted that Braunschwein and Dulles were somehow involved in the smuggling. They'd made too much of an effort to get him into the Great Cave tonight. And what was more, Michael was certain that, despite the storm, they were expecting the plane. Now, more than ever, he needed to be careful.

Soon Michael came to the little hill. It was pitch dark, much earlier than usual. The view from the top was not nearly as good as it had been the last week. Not only was there no longer a full moon, but the pouring rain reduced his visibility significantly.

While he waited, Michael wondered if the plane would be able to land or take off in this awful weather. And if it was able to land, would it be able to continue on its journey?

Then, over the screaming wind, Michael heard a soft humming. The plane was much earlier than before - maybe that had something to do with the storm. Michael wondered where the others could be. And then, as if he had pressed the button with his thoughts, he saw lights flash on at both ends of the landing strip. The boy was surprised the others were already here. Over the roaring storm, he hadn't heard the cars arrive. And this time, it was impossible for him to see the source of the lights. The rain prevented him from seeing any details, even with his binoculars.

Then he heard the plane prepare for landing. First, the sound diminished, and then it came back, louder. The plane was definitely approaching. The roar of the engine became louder and louder. The plane seemed to have some difficulty aiming for the landing strip. Now the craft was coming straight at him. At the very last moment, the pilot went up again. It rushed over Michael, barely above the ground. Had the pilot turned up one second later, the machine would have burrowed right into the hill.

Michael realized it would be tough for the pilot to land safely in this stormy weather. Because the wind came from the side, the plane was constantly blowing off the strip. Would the pilot make another attempt?

At the end of the runway, two men watched the failed landing, completely bewildered.

"That was a close one; we almost had to sweep up all the cocaine!" one of them said.

"Sweep up?" the other one exclaimed. "The wind would have done it for us. Then the stuff would have been all over the island. Let's hope the pilot can land this time. Or else we'll be in big trouble tonight."

The man hadn't even finished speaking when the sound of the engine once again grew louder. The two of them saw the beam of the floodlight coming straight towards them, swinging constantly left and right.

"Let's hope it will touch down where there's concrete," one of the men shouted. Finally, one of the wheels touched down on the landing strip, but the wind lifted the plane again. Thirty feet further away, the same wheel touch touched the ground a second time. For a moment, it looked like the plane was in danger of toppling, but the pilot was able to straighten it just in time. Then, the second wheel touched down. The worst was over. As soon as the tail wheel started spinning, the pilot could put on the brakes. Less than twenty seconds later, the plane came to a stop.

All lights were turned off. The pick-up drove up and quickly positioned itself next to the tail of the plane. The pilot jumped down from the cockpit. He walked over to the fatter of the two men.

"They're nuts, these bosses of ours. Completely nuts," he yelled. "They'll send us straight into a hurricane, just to sell their stuff. From now on, they can count me out. After this load, I'm not flying another mile!"

"What are you talking about, Pedro?" one of the men asked. "You can't stay here! The storm's just getting started. What we're experiencing now is only a little breeze compared to what's to come. If this hurricane passes by us tomorrow, that plane of yours will be nothing more but a pile of scrap metal."

"Are you crazy?" the pilot exclaimed. "You think I'm planning on staying here? Give me that kerosene and you'll get your cargo. I'm flying back as soon as I can."

"That's not what we arranged," the fat man shouted. "We only have to give you your fuel. There's no way we want anything to do with that stuff. Come on, get out of here; your tank is almost full. You can leave!"

"Not so fast, buddy," the pilot said. "You know you're responsible for the results of each flight to the States. For this, they're paying you handsomely. You know just as well as I do, that I only have a slight chance of being able to take off with such a strong crosswind. The cargo is way too heavy for that. I'll be happy if I can get airborne in an empty plane. And, you know your life won't be worth a nickel if that cargo goes missing because of your own stupidity."

Braunschwein did know all too well that the pilot was right. To take off with an overloaded machine in these weather conditions, would be pure suicide. When the big bosses would learn that a cargo worth millions was lost because of his stubbornness, he could kiss his pleasant little life goodbye. So he ordered the cocaine to be taken from the plane.

From the hilltop, Michael had watched the landing take place. While the plane was standing still, he'd been debating about what he should do. He could wait here safely until the plane took off, or sneak up closer. He'd seen the two men argue, but he didn't know what it was about. He also wanted to be sure Braunschwein and Dulles were indeed involved in the smuggling. Once he saw the drugs being transferred to the pick-up, he could not keep his curiosity in check any longer. Very carefully, Michael crept down the hill. Covered by the bushes along the landing strip, he inched closed and closer. He couldn't have done this last week. Not only had it been deadly quiet, but the whole area had been lit by the moonlight.

When he was only about thirty feet away, he recognized Braunschwein's and Dulles's voices. What Michael suspected was finally confirmed. The two gentlemen were not only local dignitaries, they also lent a hand to a drug smuggling operation.

For now, Michael knew enough. He got ready to slowly steal away, when he heard Dulles's voice again.

"You got any idea," he asked Braunschwein, "where we can stow this load as safely as possible?"

"Not around the hotel, that's for sure," the other one said. "I don't want to take that risk. How about the Stemman villa? That's in an isolated spot, it's a sturdy house, and the owner isn't here right now. As soon as that plane leaves, we'll get the keys to the house. They're at the hotel."

Michael heard more than he could have hoped for. While all eyes were on the plane that was starting to move with its engine roaring, the boy disappeared into the bush.

TWENTY-THREE

Patricia had been waiting for her son for more than a hour. The Great Cave was fixed up quite domestically, under the circumstances. Someone brought a light generator. With its one thousand watt power, the machine was capable of lighting all the nooks and crannies of the cave. On the sections higher up, people had spread out long strips of plastic foil, so they could make their beds on them. As the evening progressed, more and more people gravitated towards the cave. The latest reports on the radio said the storm's power was increasing by the hour. It may have been three hundred miles away, but right now it was headed straight for the island. If it didn't veer off course, which was always a possibility, they could expect Delphine by tomorrow afternoon.

Although it wouldn't be absolutely necessary to seek shelter in the cave until the morning, many inhabitants had made the choice to spend the night there. They were mainly elderly people, women, and children. They would rather be safe than sorry. In small clusters, they discussed the situation. Some tried to distract themselves with a book. But nobody felt like going to sleep. And certainly not Patricia. She couldn't understand why Michael was staying at Johnny's for such a long time. It was too bad everybody had taken down their antennas or she definitely would have contacted the Rogers family by radio a long time ago.

Patricia thought perhaps she should go over to their house, but that wouldn't make much difference. Perhaps Johnny's parents had also decided to spend the night in the Great Cave. In which case, Michael would be waiting for them to get ready, so he could go with them in their Land Rover. That must be it, she told herself. They'll all be coming in together later on.

Not a minute later, Patricia's face brightened. She saw the Rogers family enter the cave with their luggage. But her relief vanished when she realized that her son was not with them.

From the moment he left the airport, Michael wondered what he should do. At first he intended to get to the Great Cave as quickly as possible. He knew his mother would be anxiously waiting for him there. But it wasn't really that big of a detour to pass by Stemman's house for a minute. Of course, he thought, there are risks, but, so far, everything had gone well. In just a short time, he'd learned a lot, and that should have been enough, but he still wanted to be absolutely certain the load of cocaine would be delivered to exactly that location.

In the end, his eternal curiosity got the better of him. Or was he still motivated by the search for his father?

It was just a fifteen-minute walk from the airport to Stemman's house. On the way back he did not want to cross the little bridge. That was much too dangerous. If they wanted to ambush him, that would be the best spot. So, he got into the water some three hundred feet from there. It only came up to his waist, so it was easy for him to wade to the other side. From there he continued his trip.

It wasn't until he reached the higher ground that he was able to see how violent the storm had become. The slender stems of the palm trees bent all the way over to one side. Some had snapped or were uprooted already. The screaming wind pressed the palm leaves together into bundles. Coconuts were falling from the trees. Michael tried to imagine how these beautiful trees would look after the storm.

Finally, he saw Stemman's villa looming in the distance. It was only a few weeks ago that he and Johnny ate mangos in the garden, so this area was familiar to him. He knew the house was close to the water on top of a cliff that dropped straight down to the ocean.

At the driveway, Michael stopped. From here he could hear the swirling water. Around the villa itself, he could not detect anything suspicious. Unexpectedly, Michael got scared. Was it possible he misunderstood? After all, there were dozens of abandoned houses around here. The boy couldn't restrain himself any longer and cautiously slipped into the garden.

Several times he heard coconuts thudding on the ground around him. The villa was still completely closed up. It would be hard to bring the load inside. He didn't think they could remove part of the storm fence in such a strong wind. But then Michael remembered the garage. Most likely, they'd driven the whole pick-up loaded with the drugs inside and parked it in the garage. That wouldn't have taken more than a few minutes. That meant, they were gone by now then. That's how they did it, he thought. And that's why it was so quiet.

Quickly, Michael felt much more at ease. However, he didn't want to leave until he made sure the load was inside the garage. Was there a place where he could see inside? He couldn't open the gate. Michael snuck around the side of the garage.

There was one tiny window. It was covered with a storm panel, but to the side there was a narrow one-inch crack. The boy got out his flashlight and shined it inside. At once, a feeling of blissfulness washed over him. The beam of the light revealed the pick-up with the tied down packages of cocaine. The boy could hardly suppress a cry of victory. Mission accomplished, he thought proudly.

Slowly he turned around, but suddenly his upper arm was grabbed roughly. In the beam of the flashlight he was holding, Michael saw Braunschwein's bloated face, giving him a surly look.

TWENTY-FOUR

At the same time, in Nassau …

"Sir, we're very sorry, but it is absolutely no use to inquire about tomorrow morning's flight. The hurricane is expected to be hitting Long Island by then. All flights over the Bahamas were cancelled this afternoon. Sir, I'm afraid you'll have to wait a few days before you can travel to Long Island. But, on a positive note, not every tourist gets a chance to experience a hurricane up close."

To John Scarecrow it was scant consolation. He was needed on Long Island now more than ever. Until this morning, his trip had run very smoothly. But just before the last leg he got stranded. Now he was stuck in Nassau for at least two days. If Delphine kept racing westward, she would cut across the northern part of Long Island. Chances were, all of the new development would get destroyed. From there, the hurricane could go in any direction. However, if she kept going in the same direction, Cuba would be the next victim and then the danger would be over for Nassau and the rest of the Bahamas. In that case he might be able to charter a plane by tomorrow evening or the day after. Scarecrow sighed. He hoped he would not be too late … or else, the consequences would be significant.

When Patricia learned from Johnny that Michael hadn't even stopped at their house, she lost it. She grabbed her bag, her rain slicker, and her flashlight, and immediately set out to find her son.

However, at the exit one of the hotel clerks stopped her. She knew him. She had seen this guy in Braunschwein's entourage.

"Sorry, Ms. O'Neil," he said. "We've received official orders. Nobody is to leave the cave. It's already dark out and the storm has gotten so severe that it's too much of a risk to venture outside. Especially without a vehicle. It's for your own safety."

"I have to find my son," she shouted. "And nobody is going to stop me!"

Patricia was seething. How dare that skinny nitwit! Didn't he realize a lioness looking for her cub could be life-threateningly dangerous?

She raised her arm to hit the man in the head with her light, but before she could do anything, she felt a hand grab her wrist. Abruptly, she turned around. Patricia stood face to face with Roby, one of the few people on this island she still respected tremendously.

"Don't do it, Patricia," he said in a quiet voice. "Don't do anything you'll regret later on."

His fatherly expression immediately disarmed her. Sobbing, she fell into his arms.

"I'm so scared," she sniffled. "What if something happened to Michael? He should have been here ages ago. Something's gone very wrong."

"Patricia," he answered calmly. "Michael is certainly someone who can take care of himself. He's in his element in these forces of nature. He was born and raised among it. No wonder he seeks it out. And if he does get into trouble, don't forget he has special powers at his disposal. He'll get the kind of help other people can never even consider. No, you have to trust him. He'll be all right."

With these wise words, Roby calmed Patricia down. Even so, Roby hoped he wasn't wrong.

"So the little man wanted to be a big detective. But he forgot that you have to keep your wits about you when you're dealing with the likes of Mr. Braunschwein."

The fat man's voice was taunting. Michael crouched with his back against the garage door. Braunschwein held Michael's upper arm in an iron grip. Next to him, the gigantic Dulles stood laughing mockingly.

"You don't have such a big mouth anymore, do you?" Braunschwein asked. "Now you listen to me. Before I finish with you, I'll satisfy your curiosity big time. Your father had the same nasty habit of meddling in my affairs. He should have been occupying himself with those dolphins elsewhere. He didn't realize that he wasn't just crossing me, but the big drug bosses too. We never intended to make big money through the hotel and the development; that was just a cover; we needed a base for an important smuggling route. Who cares about tourists if we take in a hundred times more with drugs? But your dad constantly got us into trouble. And that was before we started this smuggling operation. You've got to get rid of someone like that fast. And so we did."

Michael was shocked. His suspicions were actually true.

"But we did a really clean job," Braunschwein explained. "We don't like to get our hands dirty. We leave that to the experts. The day you were born, your father was the victim of the perfect diving accident. We flew in John Scarecrow from the States especially for the job. He is a real professional. He comes and he vanishes and nobody notices him, all while providing a very credible accident. Only last time, he ran into a bit of bad luck. Without meaning to, Scarecrow got mixed in with a Colombian drug gang – rivals of ours – and he got caught. However, a few days ago, we finally got him out of prison. If this hurricane arrived just a little later, you and your mom could have met him. I even offered you one last chance: you could have gone to the Great Cave."

Braunschwein's voice dropped even lower.

"No, you're worse than your father. You had to go to that airport. Well, you brought this on yourself. Now you know too much. Behind that wall, there's a load of cocaine worth thirty million dollars. I'd be nuts if I waited for Scarecrow to get here. Tomorrow, he can keep himself busy with your mother. Just this once, we'll be forced to get our hands dirty, although this hurricane makes it real easy for us, isn't that right, Charlie?"

All this time, Michael kept his eye on the two men. But Braunschwein's iron grip didn't loosen for a second. Michael knew he had to break free and flee, but he didn't know how or even where to go. But why escape anyway? The giant would catch up with him in no time. Then the solution flashed through his mind: the ocean. Even though it was a churning mass, it was his only hope. He could swim like a fish and he was already wearing part of his diving gear. All he had to do was free himself.

Michael looked at Braunschwein's face. He'd almost finished his story. Then Michael's gaze dropped to the spot where the man's two stubby legs came together. Now he knew what to do.

As hard as he could, Michael kicked Braunschwein's orange Bermuda shorts. The boy heard what sounded like the roaring of a wounded bull. He felt his arm being released and saw how the man, groaning, jack-knifed and buckled. *Touché*, Michael thought. He ran as fast as he could narrowly passing Dulles, who looked at his boss instead of Michael.

"That rotten kid! You break his neck, and don't come back before you're done!" Braunschwein hollered.

But Michael was sprinting towards the ocean. First, straight across the lawn. Then he scrambled over the rocks until he came to the edge of the cliffs. Below him, some fifty feet down, the waves crashed against rocks. Michael turned and saw Dulles charging after him. The boy took a deep breath, and with a running start, jumped into the swirling mass of water.

When he resurfaced, he saw Dulles standing at the edge of the abyss. Then, what Michael least expected, happened. At first the giant man hesitated, but then he bent forward and jumped after Michael. Michael tried to dive so he could come up as far from his pursuer as possible. He was hoping Dulles would lose sight of him in the water. But no matter how hard he tried, Michael couldn't go under. He remembered he was wearing his diving suit; it was keeping him afloat. He started swimming away as fast he could, but the giant had ended up in the water not less than fifteen feet away from him. The man kept a steady gaze on Michael and swam towards him in powerful strokes. In spite of Michael's efforts, the distance between him and the man chasing him grew smaller and smaller. Michael was paralyzed with fear. If Dulles grabbed him, he would never be able to free himself.

Michael started shaking all over. Those vibrations traveled under the water. When Dulles finally grabbed his ankle, Michael screamed. He had one last chance to suck in air before Dulles pushed him under. The giant's thighs pressed against his body. Michael was stuck.

Instinctively, he held his breath, but he was exhausted. He couldn't keep going much longer. If he tried to gasp for air again, he would take in water and suffocate.

Suddenly, Michael remembered his diver's knife. With one hand he tried to reach his leg, but the giant's thighs prevented him from reaching his weapon. He tried with his other hand, but he still couldn't reach it.

Just when he was starting to choke, he saw a gray silhouette flash past. The next moment, Dulles was pushed aside roughly and his legs lost their grip. Michael broke through to the surface of the water, gasping for air. He heard the man howling. He turned around and saw Dulles groaning in pain. Then he saw a dolphin fin racing cutting through the water at full speed, charging the giant. Dulles screamed again.

Now Michael understood what was happening. He recognized Derby, his dolphin brother. No doubt Derby had heard him and had come to his rescue. Fortunately, Michael did not see it, but he knew Dulles was in the water with his belly ripped open. The dolphin had rammed Dulles several times with his pointy snout. The first time was in his side, which had most likely torn his liver. The second time was the lethal blow, full in the stomach. Michael knew that dolphins killed sharks this way.

Then Derby came to him. Michael embraced his brother and thanked him. He clutched the dolphin's dorsal fin with both hands and was immediately taken in tow.

Only now did Michael notice how savagely the ocean was heaving. One moment, he was on top of a wave, the next it looked as if he would be buried under a wall of water. Those waves had to be ten or fifteen feet high. It was certainly turning out to be an adventure. No carnival could ever offer anything like this. Michael felt safe having Derby with him. The water was warm and his diving suit gave him extra protection against the cold.

Michael started to worry though. Out here in the ocean, he was out of danger for the time being, but he couldn't stay here the whole night. Roby told him there would be thirty to forty-five feet high waves once the hurricane passed through. How would he be able to keep going? Maybe even a dolphin couldn't cope. No, he had to try to get ashore and find a safe haven, but that wouldn't be easy. Where could he get his feet on solid ground without being crushed by the breakers? Ten to fifteen feet high waves, crashing violently against the rocks, nobody could survive that. In the distance, Michael listened to the roar of the breaking waves; he could barely hear it over the howling wind. And the wind was picking up by the minute.

Michael had no doubt about it; the hurricane was definitely heading straight for the island. He would only be able to get on land safely where the coast was completely shielded. He would have to hurry too! Right at that moment, Mr. Powell and Columbus's log flashed through his mind. Five hundred years ago, the explorer had already found the ideal spot. Now, he could benefit from this knowledge. He had to get to the inlet with the little island in front of it.

The boy spurred on the dolphin, who started dragging him through the water at a high speed. Michael felt the friction. He hoped his arms would not cramp up because they still had much to endure.

During the wild journey, they passed a coast that looked particularly sinister. Michael thought of Dulles. The surf would continuously fling the body of his opponent against the rocks until there would be nothing left. He also thought of his mom, who was at the cave, undoubtedly in a panic. And then he thought of Braunschwein. It would be best not to run in to him again tonight. But for now he didn't need to worry. There was no way Braunschwein could have witnessed the scene with the dolphin. The water was too dark and wild, and the man was too high up. Surely, he would think Michael didn't survive. That was for the best, but that was also why Michael probably shouldn't go to the cave tonight. No, he had to find another hiding place where he could spend the next twenty-four hours safely. But where? He couldn't knock on anybody's door. By now, all the residents had probably set up camp in the Great Cave. And in the next village, everybody would be in the church.. If he could even make it that far, they wouldn't let him in. And breaking into a home was useless. The whole day, everybody had been working hard to lock everything up. And would those houses be able to withstand the hurricane anyway?

Suddenly, he heard the thundering crash of the surf in the distance. Michael and Derby were approaching the rocky little island that, for the most part, shielded the entrance to the dolphin inlet. Gigantic waves were breaking on it. Foam splashed up sixty feet in the air. Just in front of the two entrances, the water was churning. The current had to be terribly strong. But Michael had no choice. Derby slowed down. Fortunately, the animal knew this place very well.

The closer they got, the stronger Michael felt the impact of the hurricane. He was hoping Derby would be able to stay on course, and that his muscles wouldn't give out. Otherwise, the surf would definitely smash him against the rocks. Holding his breath, clinging to the animal with all his might, Michael hoped for the best.

They made it! Once they had passed through the channel, the surf lessened significantly. It took the dolphin less than a minute to reach the far end of the inlet. Still, the waves kept rolling up to the beach. But here they were no higher than five feet.

Michael knew the moment had come to let go of Derby. The boy embraced the dolphin and waited for a fresh wave. When it came, he started swimming as fast as he could. The surf lifted him and rolled toward the beach. Michael felt as if he was riding a surfboard.

Suddenly, he was on solid ground and the wave washed over him. He stayed down on the hard sand for a few seconds until the water had almost completely receded. Then, he quickly hopped to his feet and ran up the beach, chased by another wave.

Exhausted, Michael flopped down on the wet sand. Everything Jason had taught him a few weeks ago had helped save him.

Michael stood in front of the Hotel Columbus, which was all locked up. The ocean had almost reached the building. It wouldn't be long before the waves would be pounding its walls. He couldn't risk using it as a safe haven. And he couldn't stay and rest here for too long, either. The wind howled terrifyingly and the rain came down in buckets.

Then it hit him. Michael was a little frustrated he hadn't thought of this earlier: the lighthouse! It was only about a half a mile away. Where better to brave the hurricane than inside a chunk of concrete? And furthermore, that way he would be very close to his own father. Michael hoped the salt had sufficiently eaten away at the tower's lock, so that he could open the gate quickly.

Encouraged, Michael stood. For the first time he felt how sore his muscles were, but he didn't care. Soon, he was trotting along the beach, or, what was left of it. In many places the water came up to the shrubs. Again, he noticed that the palm trees bowed to the ground, if they weren't already uprooted or broken. More coconuts were coming down, thudding around him. He was careful to avoid them, but sometimes they fell without warning. When the tower came into view, Michael picked up several of the coconuts. The ocean water had made him thirsty and who knew how long the hurricane would go on. He was happy he still had the energy bars on him too.

At last he reached the spit of land where the lighthouse stood. He noticed the waves already reached the bottom of the structure, but because the base was made out of an enormous block of concrete, it didn't do any harm. The concrete could withstand much more.

As Michael climbed the stairs, he had to make a serious effort to not be blown away. When he got to the gate, he put down the coconuts and pushed against the metal. As he had expected, it didn't move. He quickly descended the stairs. A moment later Michael returned, this time carrying a huge boulder. His heart was in his throat. What if he couldn't open the gate?

But he didn't want to think about that. Using the boulder as a battering ram, Michael gave the gate a first blow, hitting the lock as hard as he could. Sorry, Dad, he thought, but I'm sure you won't be mad about this. He tried again.

And as if his father was listening to him, the lock gave way after the third bang. The gate flew open. Michael lost his balance and tumbled, boulder and all, into the lighthouse. It was pitch black. But, when he switched on his flashlight, he saw he couldn't have found a better hiding place. He was in a round space about six feet in diameter, without a single window. Other than a thin layer of sand, there was nothing on the floor. Directly opposite the entrance, a ladder hung on the wall. It led up to another floor. Michael clasped the flashlight between his teeth and climbed up. With his hand he pushed up the hatch and peered inside. Right away he saw two chests. The rest looked similar to downstairs, just a bit smaller. Furthermore, the ground was much dryer and the walls had two tiny windows. Looking at the chests up close, he saw they were locked. There would be time to investigate later on.

Michael decided to spend the night in this part of the lighthouse, but first he gathered more coconuts so he would have enough to drink. With the last of his strength Michael rolled another big boulder up the stairs. It barely fit through the doorway. Finally, Michael pushed the gate closed and blocked it with the two boulders. No gust of wind could wrest it open. When he was finished, Michael realized he lacked the strength to pick open even one of the coconuts.

Satisfied, Michael laid down against the chests. As far as he was concerned, the hurricane could go ahead. He was ready for it. As soon as he closed his eyes, Michael fell asleep.

TWENTY-FIVE

Wednesday, August 26

Around seven o'clock in the morning, the following report came over the radio:

Hurricane Delphine has reached its maximum strength. The storm is moving west at a speed of twelve miles-per-hour. The hurricane has a force of at least one hundred miles-an-hour, with gusts of wind reaching one hundred and twenty miles-per-hour. At sea and along the coast, the waves are expected to be thirty to fifty feet high. The hurricane will reach the northern part of Long Island within a few hours. All inhabitants are advised to stay indoors from now on. The weather service expects the storm to be pushing on in the direction of Cuba. More information about the hurricane in one hour.

In the Great Cave, not a sound was heard. Everyone was horrified by the weather report. The hurricane was still following the same path; it was headed straight for them. They feared the worst for their possessions.

At midnight, the last residents had arrived in the cave. Braunschwein. Nobody was missing, except Michael O'Neil and Charlie Dulles. Everybody was wondering what could have happened to those two. In this terrible weather, the only safe place to be was in the cave. Even a house could no longer offer protection. Through the cave's opening they could see how violently the forces of nature were raging. Although it was daytime, the sky remained as dark as night. The rain was still coming down in torrents. The wind was blowing ferociously and was ravaging the remaining shrubs and trees. The plants were shaking mercilessly. Long trails of leaves swirled by as if it was fall. Thick branches snapped off like twigs. Sturdy trees creaked and groaned. Many bushes flew past, flapping in the wind as if they were newspapers.

At that same moment, a mile and a half to the north of the cave, Michael woke up. He'd been hearing the repeated, muffled bangs for a while, but because he was asleep, they hadn't really registered. Only after the last bang did he finally wake up. It was as if a giant fist was pounding the lighthouse. The boy went to the little window facing north. It was eight inches wide and consisted of thick glass anchored in the lighthouse wall. At first he didn't see anything because of a thick layer of dust. He wiped the glass clean with his wet handkerchief. Then it all became clear. A humongous wave came rolling straight at him. Michael guessed it was least thirty feet high. With no trouble at all, the flood of water washed over the mass of rocks between the ocean and the lighthouse. The wave lost much of its force. Yet it was still a ten-foot wall of water that slammed against the foot of the lighthouse and crashed open at the concrete base. The building shook and the glass was completely drenched by the ocean. Michael was shocked by all this violence of nature. Was this the worst part or was it just the beginning?

Michael walked over to the window on the other side. After he had wiped it too, he could hardly believe his eyes. The beach he'd walked on just last night was completely gone. Everything had turned into ocean, and one giant wave after another came rolling in. Each wave greedily forced its way onto land. The spot where he'd picked up the coconuts was full of uprooted palm trees. Retreating waves dragged them out to sea, but then the next wave pushed the trunks back up and used them as battering rams for another attack. One tree after another was crushed. Michael saw that the water now consisted of pieces of palm trees, shrubs, chunks of coral, boulders, and sand. The destructive power of the surf had increased tremendously. No, he would no longer be able to perform a landing such as last night. Not even in the dolphin bay. There, too, gigantic waves would be pounding the hotel. Suddenly, Michael thought of Derby. His dolphin would be far from the coast, safely out in the open ocean. At least Michael hoped he was.

Another blow brought the boy back to reality. Michael wanted to know what the situation was downstairs. He opened the hatch and switched on his flashlight. Thanks to the two boulders the gate was still closed, but there was about three inches of water inside. Each time one of those huge waves crashed on to the lighthouse, it squeezed a little water through the cracks. It was good to be dry on the first floor. Michael was also glad the gate was located where it was. Otherwise, it would long have collapsed under the pressure of the water.

Michael regretted that he didn't have a radio. Now he couldn't get any information about the course of the storm. He remembered Roby's words: up to fifty feet high waves. Would it really get that bad? And would the lighthouse hold up? Under the circumstances, all he could do was wait and hope for the best.

Michael fixed his attention on the chests. He tried to lift one, but barely succeeded. It couldn't have been an easy job to haul them through the narrow lighthouse opening. Each chest was locked. Michael was lucky to have his diver's knife on him. Maybe he could use it to pry them open, but before he got started, he wanted to have breakfast.

The boy grabbed a coconut and pressed it between his left hand and his right knee. He'd tried to pick young coconuts because they contained more coconut milk and were easier to open up. With a steady hand, Michael used his knife to chip at the top of the green nut. As he went deeper, he worked more carefully. Finally, a small black hole was visible in the white coconut flesh. He'd done it. He turned the tip of the knife around in the little opening a few times until it was big enough. Then, he enjoyed the sweet liquid.

When Michael was finished, he took out the energy bars he'd stashed in the pouch pocket of his rain slicker. The foil wrapping thankfully had remained undamaged. Michael decided to eat two of the bars. He was very hungry. He would save the other two and only use them when he really needed to.

After he'd emptied a second coconut, he decided to get started on those chests. It looked like they'd been standing here for a long time, most likely years. They were made of metal, now very rusty. Only in a few places could Michael see that originally they were painted blue or green. But the padlocks had not been affected by time. His knife wouldn't do much good. But the ring holding the padlock seemed like it might be weak enough.

Michael sawed the metal with the serrated part of his diver's knife. Slowly, he felt his tool sink deeper into the metal. Finally, he broke through. He yanked the padlock and wrenched the ring open further. When the lock was off, Michael pulled the latch on the lid.

As soon as he saw the inside of that first chest, Michael gasped. A long time ago, the owner had painted his name and address in blue paint on the light green background:

BENJAMIN T. JANSEN
1971 ASHBURY STREET
SAN FRANCISCO, CA 94117
USA

So these chests were his father's? Why had his mom never told him about them? Or did she not even know they existed? When were they brought here? And by whom? Maybe he would get the answers right there and then.

Michael pulled away the brown paper that lay on top of the opened chest. He saw dozens of books. He picked one up and looked at the title. It was a nature guide on corals. No doubt about it; these were definitely his father's books. These were the books that his mother had to leave behind when she moved back to the States ten years ago. When the house was rented out for the first time, Morris probably took the books and put them in a safe place. The good man must have thought the best spot for the books was where their owner was buried. When Morris died, went the secret of where the books were stored went with him to his grave. That was the most logical explanation.

Whatever the case, Michael was glad he'd recovered the books. He had no doubt that the other chest would have the same contents: books on the ocean, diving, tropical islands, and, especially, books on dolphins. The books on dolphins were all grouped together. One by one, Michael took them out. Some had magnificent color illustrations. In many places he saw his dad's handwriting - proof that he'd studied them seriously.

One of the last books Michael opened was about the birth of dolphins and how to take care of young dolphins in captivity. He saw a piece of paper folded in half pushed into the book's dust jacket. Michael took it out and unfolded it. On this page his father had written a whole text in beautiful penmanship. And when Michael started reading it, he felt a jolt.

Statement

Herewith I, the undersigned Benjamin T. Jansen, born in San Francisco, on October 7th, 1946, recognize paternity of the child fathered by me in November or December of last year with Patricia

O'Neil, born in Boston, on April 12th, 1956, and which will be born of her in August or September of this year. Herewith, I also declare that this child will be my sole heir.

Signed on January 15th, 1978.
Benjamin T. Jansen.

Michael could hardly believe his eyes. This was the will his mom thought was lost. It would mean an end to their money troubles. He would be allowed to take his father's name, and the twelve houses, plus the house on Long Island, would be theirs. With the inheritance, Michael and his mother could live without any worries. This was fantastic news. Now, all he had to do was to get out of this storm alive.

Michael suddenly realized that he no longer heard the howling wind. And the pounding and splashing of the water seemed lighter as well. Michael went back to the window. Not one tree was moving. The world was as quiet as a mouse. The sky was a bright blue, and not a single drop of rain was falling, but the waves were still huge and smashing against the beach. The hurricane itself was now over though. So, there was no reason to stay in the lighthouse any longer. He wanted to find his mom as soon as possible to tell her the good news. But he still had to watch out for Braunschwein.

Michael slid the precious document back into the dust jacket and stuffed the book in the pouch pocket of his slicker. He bounded down the iron stairs. He rolled the two boulders to the side and opened the gate. Between two rushing waves, Michael spurted away from the lighthouse on to the beach.

Only now he could clearly see the damage the storm had done. The beach, normally fine white sand, was now littered with chunks of coral and smashed-up palm trees. He had to climb over them every few feet. The beach was an obstacle course. The way back was going to be much more trouble than he had anticipated, but he didn't care – nothing could ruin his happiness.

Until the wind picked up. At first it was simply a light gust, but then a stronger one followed, and then an even stronger one. Michael looked at the sky and gasped. The bright blue sky was literally becoming erased by a wall of ink-black clouds. They were coming at him like an enormous herd of wild horses.

"The eye!" Michael shouted like a madman. "The eye of the hurricane! How could I be so stupid? Roby had warned me about this!"

Michael turned around and ran as if the devil was chasing him. He raced toward the lighthouse as fast he could. He was at least a quarter mile away. Every second the wind was getting stronger, and then it started to rain again. On top of this, tree trunks and boulders were blocking Michael's way. The wind changed direction, so now the rain pelted his face.

In no time, Michael was drenched again. There was no sign of a blue sky. He could barely keep going. The wind was so powerful, Michael was afraid he might not make it.

Michael cursed himself. He felt his strength slipping away. He couldn't fight the storm for much longer. Fortunately, he was almost there. And it looked like he was going to make it.

But, it was too soon to start cheering. Just as Michael crept across the last boulder and was about to descend, he lost his footing. He slid down on his stomach and landed in the sand. Quickly, Michael got to his feet, and not a moment too soon. A wave came rushing in. Suddenly, he was up to his waist in water. The palms of his hands and his knees were scraped and his rain slicker was torn. But now the path to the lighthouse was clear. With a last effort, Michael ran across the rocks. He stopped to wait out a rolling wave. Then, he sprinted the last part, up the stairs and into the lighthouse. He was just in time, too. A new mass of treacherous water engulfed the base of the tower.

Michael closed the gate once again and he climbed upstairs. For the second time in less than twelve hours, he dropped down exhaustedly. He was mega lucky. Another hundred yards and he would've been a goner. And Roby had explained it to him so clearly. When the core of the hurricane passes by, it will be calm for a while, but it's a deceptive calm. Michael looked at his bleeding hands, at his chafed knees, and finally at his torn rain slicker. And then, then he screamed. He collapsed, crying. The pouch pocket of his rain slicker was torn open and the book with the valuable document had disappeared!

TWENTY-SIX

Thursday, August 27

The sun had been up for half an hour. For the first time in several days, the sky was blue again, only an occasional little cloud drifted by. The wind was still sharp at times, but Delphine had definitely left the Bahamas behind. She was now over Cuba. If the hurricane kept going the same route, it would reach the Gulf of Mexico that afternoon. America would have to prepare for the worst.

During her passage through the Bahamas, Delphine was especially destructive in the northern part of Long Island. The famed Hotel Columbus is completely flattened. This was due in part to the wind, but primarily from the huge waves, which ultimately leveled it. The residents of the nearby development have lost most of their possessions. All wooden houses have been completely destroyed. Almost all stone houses have lost their roofs. Only a small number of residences in the southwestern section of the development have escaped the havoc caused by Delphine. Fortunately, very few people were hurt, thanks to the fact that all inhabitants had made their way to the Great Cave, a refuge where they were perfectly safe from the heavy weather. At the time this newspaper went to press, only two persons were missing.

John Scarecrow folded his newspaper. When he tried to read on a small airplane, it never took long before he felt sick. He was better off looking at the clouds.

He'd left at dawn. He'd had a hard time convincing the pilot, but eventually the stack of dollars sealed the deal. Last night, Scarecrow received a call from Braunschwein. Scarecrow was expected urgently. "Highjack a plane if you have to," Braunschwein screamed at him. His assistant had been killed. And the little brat who knew everything, had turned up again. His mother found him at home. Their house had been one of the few the hurricane had spared. She'd left the cave early in the evening when the worst of the storm was over to see if that kid of hers had been hiding out there. And, what do you know, there he was! It was a good thing those two were holing up in there at the moment. Before one of them even had even the slightest chance to contact other people, they both had to be wiped out. That meant Scarecrow couldn't spare any more time. If he arrived on Long Island early this morning, he could finish the job. Then, they would be rid of those troublemakers for good.

From a distance, John Scarecrow saw the island slowly getting closer. From the plane, it looked peaceful. It was hard to tell from this distance that it was destroyed in many places. Not until the plane flew over the north shore could Scarecrow and the pilot survey the enormous damage. Almost none of the palm trees were in one piece. The beaches were strewn with snapped off trunks. Where the Hotel Columbus had been, there was now only shapeless rubble. The many houses along the Atlantic coast were heavily damaged. But John Scarecrow didn't have much time for sightseeing. The pilot found the landing strip between the two lighthouses and was already descending.

"Hold on tight," he shouted. "And if we end up in the bushes anyway, don't complain. I did my best. You wanted to do this!"

From way up, Scarecrow could see they'd already cleared the landing strip. The tree trunks and shrubs had been dragged to the side. Next to the strip, an old jeep was waiting for him. Where had Braunschwein dug up that old piece of junk, he wondered. But Scarecrow didn't have much time to think it over. As the plane descended, it bounced between the crosswinds. The pilot made every effort to keep his machine on course. He pressed ahead. Scarecrow had paid him too much to give up. Fortunately, this strip was pretty long, which gave him enough space to adjust.

For a few seconds, the cross winds seemed to stop. This was the moment. The pilot reduced his speed and with a slight tremor, the plane touched down.

Good job, John Scarecrow thought. This pilot had experience and he knew how to use it.

As soon as the machine came to a halt, the jeep drove up. Scarecrow climbed out of the plane and into the car. Braunschwein left as fast as he could.

"That was good," he said. "You're still as punctual as ever. But, you've changed over the years. Tell you the truth, I almost don't recognize you."

"Well, what would you expect, old man? Jail is no spa."

Braunschwein laughed out loud.

"Let's get to the point," he said. "Any idea how you're going to do it?"

"Of course; perfect planning and clean workmanship have always been my specialties."

"What should I do in the meantime?"

"If you can stomach it, you can be there. But no one else. You know I normally don't want any witnesses."

"Relax! Two of my guys are keeping an eye on them as we speak, but as soon as we get there, I'll send them packing. I just hope they're still at the house."

"Sure they are. Going through a hurricane makes you tired!"

"Tell me about it!" said Braunschwein, rubbing a sore spot.

The next moment, he turned off the main road.

"When we are three hundred yards from the house," Scarecrow

said, "we'd better stop and go on foot. This has to be a complete surprise. They can't get suspicious in any way."

"Well, then let's stop right now," said Braunschwein.

He parked the jeep in the bushes. After that, the two of them walked on silently.

Not five minutes later, they saw the house in the distance. The two men who were keeping watch appeared. Braunschwein told them to go home.

When they had left, Scarecrow turned to Braunschwein.

"Give me the key to the house and the gun with the silencer. Stay here and wait. When I give you a sign, you can come."

Braunschwein did as he was told. Scarecrow started sneaking up to the house. He tried to be as cautious as he could. The slightest mistake could have the gravest consequences.

Finally, he reached the front door. Scarecrow pulled it shut behind him. When he'd reached the entrance to the bedroom, he put the gun in his inside pocket. He didn't want to scare them right away.

But just as he was pushing the door open, he heard Patricia and Michael run across the terrace in the back. They had obviously seen him coming.

"Damn!" he swore. "They got away. I've got to do something quick, or the whole thing will be a big fiasco."

Immediately, he started chasing them. Patricia and Michael had, indeed, seen him. Because they couldn't defend themselves, fleeing was their only hope. First, they walked around the house, and then they ran onto the road. Suddenly, Braunschwein jumped in front of them. He cut off the two escapees and pointed a gun at them.

"Don't shoot," Scarecrow yelled from far away. "Leave it to me!"

"There you are," Braunschwein exclaimed. "Good thing I was here too. I think you've left some of your skills on Gorgona. You better end this fast. This little game has taken up enough of my time."

Michael and his mother were out of breath. Escaping was out of the question now.

Scarecrow reached Braunschwein's side and aimed his weapon at the pair.

"Put that piece of yours away, okay?" Scarecrow said to Braunschwein. "It makes too much noise, you know that."

"You're not going to let these birds fly the coop again now, are you?" The fat man snickered as he put away his weapon.

He didn't laugh very long though. A punch smashed his nose and a knee shoved into his big belly. For the second time within thirty-six hours, Braunschwein buckled. Before he realized what was happening, Scarecrow had snatched his weapon from the fat man and wrestled his arm behind his back.

"Scarecrow, have you gone nuts?" Braunschwein was shouting, all red in the face.

"I'm sorry, buddy," Scarecrow said mockingly. "I'm not Scarecrow. He's been dead and buried for many years."

"So, who are you?" Braunschwein stuttered.

The man with the brown beard's answer was slow and articulate.

"Benjamin Thomas Jansen."

TWENTY-SEVEN

The water in the bay was still heaving, though the wind had almost died down. Because of the hurricane, the ocean had been extremely turbulent and it would be days until the water was calm again. The swell sent in more big waves, and when they smashed against the rocks, they turned into a foamy mass. The ones that managed to penetrate the two narrow passageways into the dolphin bay, lost most of their steam.

There, at the edge of the water, Michael sat with his parents. This was the exact same spot where, fourteen years ago, Ben Jansen and Patricia O'Neil first admired the dolphins.

Earlier, they'd gone to see the remains of the Hotel Columbus. No stone was left on top of another. Delphine had done a thorough job. Plants and shrubs would do the rest. Next year, the ruin would be overgrown with a dense thicket. In the tropics, nature reclaims lost territory quickly. With that, the last traces of Braunschwein's empire would be gone for good.

That morning, things happened quickly. After they had tied up Braunschwein and hauled him into the trunk of the jeep, Michael and his parents left in the car. The boy pointed his father in the direction of the Stemman residence. It was largely wrecked, but the pickup with its valuable cargo had been left untouched. Afterward, they'd driven to the village at lightning speed, to telephone and inform the special police unit. They were the only ones whom Ben Jansen trusted.

A little before noon, the heavily armed men arrived. Braunschwein was officially arrested and the cocaine was confiscated. All of Braunschwein associates had to come in for questioning. And later on, Michael had to make a number of statements, too.

Until the police left with the crooks and their drugs, Ben Jansen didn't want to talk about himself. Patricia and Michael were bursting with curiosity to hear his story, but even when the military aircraft left for Nassau, Ben wasn't ready to begin.

It wasn't until he spent a long time in the bathroom that Ben was finally ready to tell them his story. He'd freshened up and put on one of his old suits. He'd also shaven his beard and mustache. Now Patricia recognized the man she had accompanied to the island fourteen years ago. And for the first time Michael could see for himself how much he looked like his father.

Then, they left for the dolphin bay, where at last Ben Jansen could begin to tell his story.

"As you both know," he started, "I left early in the morning on the day Michael was born. I didn't intend to go diving because I thought I'd be called up on the radio at any moment. I was going to observe the dolphins from the dinghy. However, in the marina where it was moored, I met a man who introduced himself as a journalist. The man told me he'd come here by sailboat in secret. He said he'd heard that the management of the development was making new plans to build a hotel by the dolphin bay and that he wanted to write an expose about this for a large American newspaper. He asked me if I would cooperate. Of course, I agreed. For me, this man was sent from heaven. Then he asked me if I wanted to do some diving. He needed underwater pictures of dolphins for his article. I refused. I didn't want to risk it in case Patricia went into labor. Once I was in the water, nobody would be able to contact me on the radio. But, the man insisted. The article was really important for the dolphins. Without pictures it wouldn't be half as attractive. When he saw I was having second thoughts, he suggested we go immediately in his boat, as that way we wouldn't waste much time. I could take my radio-receiver with me and we would only be diving for a very short time. I gave in and I never should have done that, but, at the time, I didn't have a clue that this so-called journalist was the notorious hit man John Scarecrow. Braunschwein gave him the assignment of getting rid of me in an 'accident.' And that's really easy to do under water.

"A little after noon, we dropped anchor near Cape Santa Maria. The ocean is seventy-five feet deep out there. We put on our diving gear and jumped into the water. Scarecrow dove in with an underwater camera to take pictures of me with the dolphins. When we reached the bottom, Derby swam up to me. He was still very young at the time and I wondered where his mother, Gipsy, could be. I followed him until he disappeared into a small cave. He was playing with me and in order to tease him, I turned on my diver's lamp, lit up the cave, and flashed it across his face. Suddenly, I felt the other diver behind me. He was leaning against me. At first, I thought he was looking over my shoulder. Instead, he was slowly closing the valve on my air tank. Derby started acting rather strangely. Before I could understand, I was out of air. I tried to turn around, but Scarecrow was hanging on to my air tank with his knees. No matter which way I turned, I couldn't reach him. I tried to pull his air regulator out of his mouth to get some air for myself. When that did not work, I threw off my weight belt and pushed up from the ocean floor. I used powerful strokes to go up. I could escape if I made it to the surface quickly. But Scarecrow had already thought of that, and tried to stop me. I attempted to grab him, but he kept clinging to my tank. I thought for sure I wouldn't reach the surface in time. I was out of breath, and not even half way up. But at that moment, I grasped a piece of rope with a little ball hanging from his gear: one of his emergency cartridges. I pulled it, and his vest immediately filled up with carbon dioxide. Because of the upward pressure he shot up to the surface like a rocket. Since I was free of him on my back, I could ascend easier and faster. At the very last second, I reached the water surface. I opened my mouth and sucked air into my lungs. I looked around and saw Scarecrow floating on the surface. He barely moved. Bloody foam came out of his mouth. I immediately knew that the tissue in his lungs had torn due to the overpressure of his ascent. In only a few seconds, Scarecrow had risen from below thirty-five feet to zero. Scarecrow probably held his breath, an unfortunate move because it almost always results in a collapsed lung. I dragged him toward the boat, even though I knew he was dying.

"I asked him why he wanted to murder me. He told me everything. But, the moment I heaved him aboard, he died. So there I was, with a dead gangster on board an unfamiliar ship. My first reaction was to call for help through my radio. I saw that Scarecrow had switched it off. Not a single call could have reached me that morning. I was about to turn the radio back on, when I realized it was much too dangerous. Even returning to Long Island wasn't safe. Not only would I put my life in danger, but yours and the baby's as well. I thought I didn't have any other choice but to go to Nassau for help. Meanwhile, I wanted leave everybody believing the 'accident' had been successful. I took off my diving gear and my orange diving suit. The dead man would take my place. Because of the accident, his face was already swollen. After having been in the water a while longer, he would be even less recognizable. And because everyone on the island was familiar with my orange equipment, I knew chances were pretty high that they would think it was me. Then, I threw his body overboard and watched it drift toward the beach. I felt terrible because I was certain I was going to miss the birth. I tried to reach Nassau as fast as I could, but everything went wrong when I encountered a Colombian sailing ship a couple of hours later."

Ben Jansen told them how he was first picked up by this Colombian drug gang and how they were busted by the Colombian police. Then, he explained how he ended up on that Colombian prison island. Michael was horrified. He couldn't understand why his dad hadn't revealed his real name.

"Oh Michael, I wanted to," he said, "but, I didn't think it was safe. I was afraid not only for myself, but for both of yours as well. In Colombia, my real name wouldn't have changed anything anyway. After all, they'd found me aboard a drug ship. Many people have been convicted because they - without even knowing it - were in possession of drugs and got caught. But if I kept using the name Scarecrow, all three of us would be safe from Brauschwein. He was convinced I was dead and he wouldn't do anything to you guys. Under the name 'Ben Jansen' they probably would have killed me in prison. I've seen that happen with my own two eyes more than once. In the meantime, I could only hope the years would pass quickly. When I was released quite unexpectedly, I was completely surprised. Then, I heard what my assignment was. I was thrilled. I was supposed to rub out my own wife and son. It was the perfect opportunity to get rid of Braunschwein once and for all.

"Then Delphine came along and messed everything up. She kept me in Nassau for two extra days, while I knew you were both in serious danger. When I arrived here this morning, I didn't want to finish with Braunschwein until I was certain you guys were out of danger. So, I waited for him to send his goons away, but I didn't expect that you were on the lookout and would flee. When I entered the house, I was going to tell you who I was, but by then, you were gone. I panicked. What if Braunschwein had gunned down the both of you?"

Ben Jansen put his arm around Patricia.

"But now it's all over," Patricia said. "We have a new life ahead of us. Everything is possible. It's almost like the clock has been turned back fourteen years." Then, she pointed at Michael. "Only now, you have the best possible assistant you could ever dream of having."

"It's too bad the dolphins left the island."

"They're back, Dad," Michael whooped. "Look, Derby and the others came back!"

Sure enough, as if the animals could hear Michael shouting, they jumped out of the water. Michael instantly identified Derby. He ran into the water like a maniac. He didn't even care that he still had his clothes on. At last, he was with his favorite animals. And this time, he wouldn't have to leave.

Patricia and Ben gazed after him. They'd finally found each other again.

Patricia smiled, noticing new similarities between father and son. But with this pair, she never knew what might happen next.

TWENTY-EIGHT

A few days after hurricane Delphine fizzled out over the state of Louisiana, the Miami Herald ran this short article:

THE REVENGE OF THE DOLPHINS?

A few months ago, this newspaper reported the shooting of Gipsy, a female dolphin near Key Largo. This domesticated dolphin was killed by a passenger on board a yacht owned by Harold Thompson, a wealthy industrialist from New York. It just so happens that Harold Thompson was a major stockholder in the Hotel Columbus, which was destroyed on Long Island last week during a hurricane.

Ten years ago, the hotel was built by a bay that was home to a group of dolphins. The arrival of the first tourists disrupted the lives of the animals so severely that the animals disappeared shortly thereafter. However, a few days after the hotel was destroyed by the hurricane, this very same group of dolphins returned to live in the bay once more.

By studying satellite photos, meteorologists have been able to see that the eye of hurricane Delphine passed right over the bay and the hotel. The strange thing is that 'Delphine' comes from the Latin delphina, *meaning female dolphin. Is this a matter of pure coincidence, or are cosmic powers at work here? In other words, is this the revenge of the dolphins?*

If you would like to give your reaction, or want more information on this book, the author or his other books, please visit *www.patricklagrou.be* or *www.dolfijnenkind.be.*